GORPP THE GRAPPLER

D. R. FEILER

For Linzee
D-F
9/5/22

SOUNDS & VOICES MEDIA, LLC

Gorpp the Grappler copyright © 2022 by Sounds & Voices Media, LLC

Cover design by RD Custom Designs

All rights reserved. No part of this book may be reproduced or transmitted without the written permission of the publisher, except in the case of brief quotations embodied in critical articles and reviews.

This novel is a work of fiction. Names, characters, places and incidents are either the product of the author's imagination or are used fictitiously. Any resemblance to persons, living or dead, from Earth to the moons of Saturn, is purely coincidental.

Published by Sounds & Voices Media, LLC

eBook ISBN: 978-1-957648-02-6

Paperback ISBN: 978-1-957648-01-9

Hardback ISBN: 978-1-957648-00-2

*Dedicated to my mom who took me to my first wrestling match.
She was out of this world.*

CHAPTER 1

GORPP, as we would come to call him, lay on the bunk in his dual-purpose submarine and space vessel deep below the currents of what Earthlings call the Bermuda Triangle. He wasn't the mastermind behind the clandestine occupation and planned invasion of Earth. Far from it. Gorpp was just a conscript assigned to pilot a small transport vessel between the supply ship above and the labyrinth of underwater caverns the invasion force now inhabited deep below the Atlantic Ocean.

The Earthlings didn't understand how the eruption of methane gases could get trapped below the water, then explode to the surface in this region of the Atlantic Ocean. Over the centuries, this phenomena had accounted for the sucking down of countless ships into a vortex under the sea. Many never to been seen again.

The seabed around the entrance to the caverns looked like a graveyard of sunken ships from different eras of Earth's seafaring history. The invaders used them as underwater landmarks. When Gorpp got off duty, he sometimes enjoyed joyriding off the coast of Cuba through the sunken remains of an ancient civilization some Earthlings called Atlantis. His single-occupancy vessel worked just as well under the water as it did in the air. A necessity where Gorpp came from.

A stone statue of a bull standing guard in front of an archway marked one of the spots he liked to idle his ship and relax, to get away from the monotony of his role in the occupation.

Swirling currents at this depth caused the seafloor to be uneven and could account for rogue waves. All these phenomena were a mystery to the planet's own inhabitants, but to Gorpp they were routine and presented no mystery, no threat.

Gorpp was something of an everyman among a highly advanced species. He wasn't held in high regard among his own, and his prospects offered little hope of improving.

What Earthlings would experience as a ten minute trip, to Gorpp was hardly noticeable. A fraction of a second. It was the repetition.

Load. Check the manifest. Blip. Unload. Check the manifest. Repeat. And hope you aren't noticed by a curious native. Then, you'd have to file an incident report, because while the aliens had little concern Earth could mount an effective defense, they were still in the clandestine phase of the occupation. Gorpp was a functionary, and the monotony of it ate like bacteria at his brain, because Gorpp had a trait very unusual to his kind. He wanted to stand out from the crowd. To be noticed.

During his assignment to the invasion of Earth, he had been living in his tiny transport vessel, alone, in the vast network of caverns below the Atlantic ocean that the occupation force called home. They'd chosen this location because it reminded them of home, and due to the history of strange happenings in these waters, the occasional sighting of one of their transport vessels could be more easily explained away.

When Gorpp was off duty, one of his hobbies became tuning his sensor equipment to pick up broadcasts from the

Earthlings. It was helpful to hear the language, and sometimes the transmissions were amusing. One night, in the Earth year 1975, he tuned in to a local television station broadcasting from Tampa, Florida.

Since months to us would go by in minutes to Gorpp, he found our schedules and cycles counterintuitive. But, he figured out that in 1975, Heavyweight Championship Wrestling from Florida broadcast from the Bayfront Armory at eight p.m. on Saturday nights, Earth time.

He didn't talk about it with any of his own kind, but Gorpp had become increasingly interested in the testosterone-fueled and hyperbolic soap opera of professional wrestling, and tuned in to live broadcasts every Saturday night. The storylines, the drama and the characters had him hooked.

To Gorpp, nothing could have been more alien.

One Saturday night, after using his vessel in its submarine mode to visit the ruins of Atlantis, Gorpp made sure to get back in time to settle in for the matches.

"Ladies and gentlemen, good evening and welcome to a special edition of Heavyweight Championship Wrestling from Florida's 'Champions Series,' live from the Bayfront Armory in beautiful Tampa, Florida. I'd like to start our broadcast tonight with an important announcement. Next Saturday night, one week from today, the Heavyweight Champion of the World will be in this very arena to defend his title!"

When he heard the World Champion would be in Tampa to defend his title right there at the Bayfront Armory, Gorpp leapt up from his bunk with a rare feeling of exhilaration.

For the first time in his life, he knew what he had to do. He also knew it would violate Rule Number One: Don't allow Earth's inhabitants to become aware of your presence on their planet. In wrestling terms, this was the "kayfabe" of Gorpp's kind. *Keep the secret.*

I mean, yes, they were here to take over the planet, but it

seemed to Gorpp that Central Command moved so cautiously, so methodically, that the occupation would never become an invasion.

Gorpp saw his chance to prove he should be advanced in rank, to show he was good for a lot more than running supplies back and forth.

Did Central Command even know the World Champion of Earth would be at the Bayfront Armory in Tampa on Saturday night?

He doubted it.

Gorpp made the decision in that moment to divert course on his next transport, go to Tampa and challenge Earth's Champion.

He would return a conquering hero or die in the attempt. Either seemed preferable to this monotonous existence.

CHAPTER 2

GORPP PUT on his standard uniform of boots and a formfitting bodysuit that shimmered an eggshell white, flecked with specks of silver. He sent his manifest confirmation to Central Command, then did what would have looked to us like a few minutes of a cross between yoga and meditation.

When Gorpp opened his eyes and looked at the monitor he saw the response from Central Command had a red flag on it. They'd responded with instructions to ensure prompt arrival due to the precious and perishable nature of the cargo he would be transporting.

Probably the vaccine they tell us we don't need but we all know they're developing, thought Gorpp. Most thought the sickness came from water pollution getting into their ventilation systems. These Earthlings just dumped their garbage, sewage, pesticides and nuclear waste right into the oceans.

The blinking red flag was a problem. If he picked up this cargo and brought it back to headquarters, he feared he would miss the matches at Bayfront Armory. Miss the chance to beat the World Champion. And that chance, he thought, may never come again.

Gorpp stared at the blinking red flag and hesitated. His

training, instincts, and force of habit all told him to pick up the "precious and perishable" cargo and deliver it faithfully, as he had always done, on time and with no questions asked.

He acknowledged the message with his neuropathic link, and the red light turned green. He was still feeling the lingering effects of his meditative state—the meditation of redundancy—but he unmoored his vessel from the docking clamps. Then, he started weaving through the maze of caverns, emerging into the sunken ship graveyard and, finally, the open ocean where he would begin his ascent into the sky.

CHAPTER 3

Gorpp later found he had no memory of the trip through the caverns or of his ascent. He had no memory of making a conscious decision, that instead of rising vertically toward the supply ship, he would bear northwest at low altitude over dry land from Boca Raton to Tampa. He didn't remember touching his small craft down on the roof of the Ambassador Hotel, next door to the Bayfront Armory, and walking in the front door.

His first conscious memory and what snapped him out of his stupor of destiny and defiance was the fact that there was no one around. No one in the lobby. No body slams or cheering crowds behind the curtains leading to the bleachers.

He wondered if he was in the right place. He saw a sign on the way in (he'd learned English—and most of Earth's other languages—before he entered our atmosphere). It read:

TONIGHT – 8:00 p.m.
Heavyweight Championship Wrestling from Florida
proudly presents
WORLD CHAMPIONSHIP MATCH
SOLD OUT!

Gorpp checked his implanted censor that kept the time and realized he'd made an error in translation. It was only about twelve-thirty in the afternoon in Tampa. He was early.

Gorpp took a deep breath and felt the anxiety in his brainwaves flush away to be replaced with relief and curiosity. He immediately realized he would benefit from the opportunity to study the battleground on which he would challenge the World Champion. It never entered his mind he could actually leave, make that cargo run and be back in time for the matches. His focus was on the matter at hand. Not another cargo run.

He couldn't help but notice the pervasive filth all around him. The density of the smells that we would recognize as sour sweat, dried blood, tobacco and spilled beer assaulted his senses. His convex, almond eyes could see the filth and mildew in cracks in the vinyl floor and peeling drywall.

He was grateful to be distracted by colorful posters lined up on the walls below a banner that read:

A TRADITION OF CHAMPIONS

The posters were from historic matches throughout the Earth years that took place here at the Bayfront Armory. A poster, yellowed from cigarette smoke and years in the humid Florida air, announced in bold letters:

IRON CLAW MARTINEZ VS. THE MASKED INVADER
"NO HOLDS BARRED – LOSER LEAVES TOWN"

Others depicted The Sheik of Arabia battling "Bruiser" Burt Cody and Chief Longbow vs. Cowboy Buddy Graham. Gorpp took in a popcorn machine, and a souvenir stand with cardboard boxes containing what he would later learn were programs, t-shirts and signed pictures of the night's featured attractions.

Gorpp parted the smoky blue curtain and looked down at the empty bleachers and the ring where all this history had taken place, where the champions of yesteryear had risen, reigned and fallen. Tonight, Gorpp thought, would be his time to rise to the challenge, to go toe-to-toe with Earth's World Champion and find out once and for all if he had what it took to conquer a world.

Gorpp descended the aluminum bleachers, the well-worn steps creaking with each footfall, until he reached the cement floor and stood with the ring looming above him. Again, the smells made him almost woozy, and his magnifying vision showed him all the crusted blood, grime and bacteria weaving their way through the ring mat, ropes and turnbuckles like their own invading army. Gorpp would hardly be surprised to learn staph infections were an occupational hazard.

He put the bacteria aside in his mind and decided to climb into the ring. If just the filthy ring unnerved him, what chance did he stand to best Earth's Champion? Gorpp reached for the rope and just as he wrapped his hand around it he heard the first human voice he'd ever heard in person.

"Who the hell are you?"

Gorpp turned to see a hunched shadow of a man emerging from a doorway at the far end of the ground level of the Armory. The voice sounded like churning gravel. It belonged to one Ernie Cantrell.

"Who the hell are you? I said. What are you doing messing around with my ring? And what's this getup you're wearing? You think you're some kind of wrestler, or just a goddamned freak?"

Faced with this barrage of questions from the man who turned out to be the owner of Heavyweight Championship Wrestling from Florida, Gorpp realized passing English grammar tests on the training portal hadn't prepared him for being berated by a legend of the territorial era of professional wrestling. But, he remembered the Earth custom of exchanging names. Gorpp said his name and Ernie, even as he hobbled closer, put his wrinkled and ruddy hands over his cauliflower ears, one hand holding a cigarette, still smoldering, which almost lit his few whisps of gray hair on fire. Gorpp said it again.

"Ok, ok!" Ernie said.

"Gork or Goat or Gorpp. Whatever the hell. Just stop saying it. It's hurting my addled old brain." Ernie, almost upon him now, got a closeup look at Gorpp.

"Good God, son. What kind of freak are you anyway? Your big old bald head's about twice the size it ought to be and your eyes are too. What's wrong with you? You got some kind of freak disease like old Maurice Tillet?"

Gorpp didn't respond.

"You ever heard of Maurice Tillet? They called him the French Angel with his big old head. He used to be the NWA World Champion. They said he had a tumor that made his bones grow all gnarled like a Live Oak root. That what you got?"

Gorpp didn't know what to say. He felt another wave of hesitation wash over him, like a hot ripple under his skin. He could feel sweat pricking his skin, and he knew he was blushing a faint greenish hue.

Doubt knocked him down to size.

He thought about the orders he'd had to ensure prompt pickup of that "precious and perishable" cargo. He realized not only had he gone AWOL and left the precious cargo to perish, he was also in the act, at this very moment, of breaking Rule Number One. And on top of it all, he had no idea how to respond to all the things this decrepit but fiery Earthling kept spewing at him.

That didn't seem to slow Ernie down one bit. Later, as Gorpp got to know him, he found Ernie felt most in his comfort zone having one-sided conversations. In fact, he tried to make sure those were the only kind he had.

As Ernie kept rambling on, Gorpp realized he'd again drifted into his meditative state where he lost time and recall. He tuned back in when he heard Ernie trying again to pronounce, or as it turned out, alter, his name.

"Gork? No, Gorpp. With a double *p* at the end. Look at you, with your big old head, and your superhero tighty whiteys. You swagger in here because you think you're gonna be a *wrassler?* You think you're a grappler? Gorpp the Grappler? Hey, that's not bad. I still got it, eh, kid?"

Gorpp didn't respond.

"Quiet type, huh? I like that. But listen, I gotta figure out if you're here to wrestle, or if you just wandered away from the Big Head Home and there's somebody I should call."

Gorpp collected himself and tapped into the destiny vein he'd felt when he saw the announcement that the World Champion would be here, "tonight at 8:00 p.m.!"

"I'm here to challenge the World Champion," Gorpp said with some conviction.

"Ha! Well, I like that. Gorpp the Grappler has some *cajones*. I like that. Son, I don't know how much you know about the *wrasslin'* business but I'm gonna go out on a limb and hazard a guess it ain't too much. What are you, nineteen? Twenty? I got work to do so I'm gonna keep this brief but here's The Wrestling Business 101, from Ernie Cantrell. First thing is, you don't just come strolling in here off the street. If you want a ticket to the show, too bad, it's SOLD OUT! Second thing is, if you want a tryout, you come back Tuesday at ten in the morning. You can wear your tights and boots there. You look perfect! Come back on Tuesday. I'll put you through the paces with one of the boys and we'll see what you can do on the mat."

Gorpp just looked at him.

"That's it," Ernie shouted. "Capice? Now get the hell out

of here. I got work to do." Ernie took a long drag on his cigarette, coughed the smoke out in Gorpp's face and waved him away like so much rubbish, but as Ernie hobbled back to his cramped and unairconditioned office, he turned to look back at the readymade gimmick that had just fallen into his lap. Ernie could see the posters:

NOT OF THIS WORLD
HAILING FROM PARTS UNKNOWN
GORPP THE GRAPPLER!

Gorpp turned and climbed the creaky aluminum bleachers back up to the lobby of the Armory, but with the old man having gone back into his office, Gorpp decided not to leave. If he couldn't challenge the World Champion tonight, this could at least be a reconnaissance mission. Perhaps he could balance some of the consequences of his insubordination with real substantive intelligence. Gorpp doubted Central Command even knew about the World Champion.

That's how out of touch they were.

He wrapped himself in the blue curtain at the back of the bleachers where he could see the ring without anyone noticing him.

For Gorpp, the Earth hours passed quickly. It wasn't long before he started to hear and see a few Earthlings file in. One yelled to another about turning on the house lights and getting someone up to the ticket window.

All of a sudden, a steady stream of Earthlings filed in like ants. A clamor accompanied the crowd, punctuated by occasional bellows and hollers and the smell of their sweat. Gorpp couldn't make much sense of it, but he could feel an electricity in the air. Primitive and bad smelling as they may be, these Earthlings could feel the anticipation of being witness to the World Champion defending his claim.

Once most of them were seated, Gorpp watched the house

lights go down so that only the ring was clearly visible below him. A middle-aged man with pronounced sideburns, in a rust-colored suit with white wingtip shoes, bellbottom pants and a Hawaiian shirt under his jacket, grabbed hold of a microphone that lowered down toward the center of the ring.

"Good evening, ladies and gentlemen. I'm Steve Levey, your host for Heavyweight Championship Wrestling from Florida, and master of ceremonies for this evening. Welcome to the Bayfront Armory in beautiful Tampa, Florida. Tonight, history will be made here again as World Champion, Black Jack Tolliver, defends his title against the Masked Marauder!"

The crowd cheered, but Gorpp could feel a rising level of inebriation and impatience moving like those swirling eddies under the Atlantic as it traveled through the room.

"But first, we have several other matches you won't want to miss. Our first bout this evening features two wrestlers making their professional debut—"

At this point, Gorpp drifted again. He'd seen dozens of matches on TV. He could see the similar patterns in the storylines and the contests, and would coast in his mind until something different happened.

He tuned back in as Levey said, "needing no introduction the world over, the undisputed Champion of the World, Black! Jack! Tolliver!"

The now fully inebriated crowd cheered the Champion, who raised the small club he called a blackjack into the air to rile them up even further. The Masked Marauder entered the Armory to boos and heckles and looked like he may have been a little apprehensive as he made his way to the ring. He jerked his head around to look this way and that as the crowd jeered and cursed. Years later, it would come out that the real Marauder had broken down by the side of I-75 with an overheated radiator in his Impala.

The man under the mask tonight was Ernie Cantrell's son, Davey. He'd been a competent amateur wrestler but he didn't have the fortitude to tough it out in the territories as a pro. But, tonight, his pops told him he needed to fill in for the Marauder, and saying "no" to Ernie Cantrell wasn't an option. Neither Gorpp nor the fans knew about the substitution until years later. On that warm summer night in 1975, all anyone at the Bayfront Armory knew was that the Marauder got his ass kicked all over the ring.

CHAPTER 4

Gorpp spent most of the next couple of Earth days in his vessel on top of the Ambassador Hotel. He didn't know whether to expect a patrol to show up and take him back to Central Command or if any of his superiors would be concerned about his absence. But no one showed up before Tuesday morning, so he scaled back down the hotel wall into the alley and made his way back to the Armory.

As he descended the bleachers in the Armory, his eyes were on a few Earthlings pacing around the ring apron, perhaps also here to audition for Ernie Cantrell.

"There he is!" came Ernie's gravel voice. "Come on down here." All eyes were now on Gorpp. "This is Gorpp the Grappler," Ernie said as Gorpp reached the bottom of the steps and joined the small group face to face. "Which one of you sumbitches has the stones to wrestle Gorpp here?"

The group of large young men looked around the room, then one stepped up from the back. "I'll give him a go." This one looked a bit older and more battle-hardened than the rest. He had short blonde hair, a faded tattoo of an anchor on his large bicep, a jagged scar that went from his temple to his jawline, and simple black trunks. He stepped through the ring ropes and looked down at Gorpp.

All eyes were again on the newcomer. "Well, son," Ernie said, "you got a great look, let's see if you can get in there and hook."

From his study of the language he knew of multiple definitions from a fishing hook to the act of prostitution but this didn't seem to fit either. Even the punch in boxing called a hook didn't quite seem to fit. He later learned that in wrestling parlance, a "hooker" meant a wrestler with real skills.

And a tough sumbitch.

But Ernie's meaning was clear enough in context. Gorpp hesitated for just a second as he noticed all the bacteria slithering along the ring ropes and the mat, but he pushed through it, grabbed the rope and hoisted himself into the ring. A few of the men below clapped and whupped as Gorpp and his human foe sized each other up.

Gorpp watched the way the man's muscles moved as he circled him. He watched his small but focused eyes. He thought about the hand-to-hand combat training he'd received before his deployment, and as he started to drift, he suddenly felt a shoulder drive into his gut, knocking him flat on his back with the Earthling on top of him.

This knocked the breath out of him and before he could recover, the man leapt up and wrapped one arm around Gorpp's neck and another under his arm. Gorpp found he couldn't move or breathe very well. He flailed his legs, but to no avail. Just as his consciousness started to slip away, he heard Ernie's raspy voice cut through the fog.

"Alright, Bobby. Let him up. Let him up."

Gorpp would learn later that Bobby hadn't been there to try out that day. He was Ernie's enforcer. The hooker that made sure no one got off of Ernie's script. And the tough guy

Ernie used to screen out the weakhearted who thought they could handle it in the *wrasslin'* business.

Bobby had let go of Gorpp and was about to depart through the ring ropes when Gorpp leapt up, grabbed him from behind, lifted him over his head and began spinning him around at a speed that made it hard for witnesses to believe what they were seeing. A blur.

Before anyone could say anything, Gorpp let go of Bobby and he flew fifteen rows into the bleachers before crashing into a pile of broken bones and dented aluminum.

Wrestlers called this move the helicopter, or airplane spin, but what Gorpp did with it, Ernie Cantrell dubbed the *flying saucer*. Throwing your opponent over the top rope wasn't a disqualification at HCW like it was in some promotions. That led to the flying saucer becoming Gorpp's signature move and a huge crowd pleaser, in spite of, or maybe because of, the not infrequent injuries to wrestlers and fans alike as Gorpp's opponents were hurled like projectiles into unpredictable parts of the arena.

Tryouts were cancelled that Tuesday. Ernie set Bobby's broken collar bone and put a makeshift cast on his broken wrist. Bobby didn't do any enforcing for several months after that. Ernie took Gorpp into his cramped office where an oscillating metal fan blew little scraps of paper around a desk cluttered with contracts, promo packages and overflowing ashtrays.

Gorpp the Grappler wouldn't make his debut as a curtain jerker. No, Ernie knew a featured attraction when he saw one, or he'd have been driven out of this cutthroat business long ago.

CHAPTER 5

Ernie and Bobby trained with Gorpp every day that hot summer of 1975. The Vietnam War finally ended, George Carlin hosted the first episode of *Saturday Night Live* and college kids at USF were listening to Pink Floyd and Lynyrd Skynyrd on their 8-track players. Meanwhile, Ernie Cantrell felt pretty sure he'd stumbled into a cushy retirement plan by the name of his greatest discovery yet: Gorpp the Grappler.

He wouldn't be the biggest guy on the roster, and his odd-shaped head and monotone were a bit off-putting to the boys in the locker room, but the crowds were gonna eat it up.

In the ring, they were finding he had uncanny reflexes and surprising strength, but his instincts were terrible. Sometimes, it seemed to Ernie and Bobby like Gorpp really did come from another world.

After a while, Ernie realized there were more than a few odd things about his new featured attraction. He always showed up in his tights, never showered, and left in them too. No street clothes. And he hardly seemed to sweat when he exerted himself. No one ever saw him getting into or out of a car. He just seemed to melt into the night. He didn't drink or horse around with the boys in the locker room. He didn't chase women. He didn't laugh or even smile. He was a good student in the ring, but an oddball to be sure, even among a bunch of misfits.

Once they got more comfortable putting Gorpp through his paces in the ring, Ernie started to wonder if this guy would ever be able to cut a promo. They might have to get him a manager with a gift for gab and let Gorpp be the strong, silent type.

CHAPTER 6

Instead of trying to train his new star-in-the-making to do interviews and promos to hype his debut, Ernie put it all on Steve Levey's shoulders. For several weeks, Levey would do a segment on each weekly broadcast hyping the imminent arrival of a new and mysterious wrestler to the territory. Levey, the anchorman of professional wrestling in Florida, did a remote taping from the street in front of the Armory, on a windy and rainy night. He'd hinted on a couple shows about the mysterious origins of this newcomer, even alluding to speculation he may be from another world.

"Some people are saying…"

The week before Gorpp's debut, Ernie had Steve interview a Tampa resident who said they'd seen strange lights in the sky ever since Levey had started reporting on the expected arrival of the mysterious new grappler. Levey called in a favor with a trusted local news anchor and got him to report on the UFO sightings, and even make allusions to the notion that if you wanted an up close look at these otherworldly visitors, you might want to be at the Bayfront Armory on Saturday night.

Gorpp the Grappler's debut as a main event special attraction sold out in one day. Gorpp wondered, but never asked, if anyone really had seen something or whether it was just a work Ernie had dreamt up to sell tickets.

He wondered if anyone back at Central Command would have to file an incident report over it. When he thought about it, it surprised him a little that no one had come to retrieve him. He didn't know what to expect because it was such a rare thing he'd done. And to them, it only seemed like he'd been gone for a minute or so, if they'd even noticed at all.

Gorpp acclimated quickly to Earth time. It moves more slowly so as to accommodate our primitive cognitive abilities. But, it also served his purposes by giving him more time here to challenge the World Champion before too much time passed at Central Command.

CHAPTER 7

The night of the match turned out to be another soggy one, with wind gusts up to forty miles an hour and the occasional tornado warning. A pretty typical forecast for a summer night in Florida, but it resulted in a more subdued crowd when they came in soaking wet. It looked like there were a few no-shows scattered throughout the bleachers, but Ernie's hype machine had done its job well enough that most fans were willing to brave the weather for a look at the mysterious visitor from parts unknown.

The ill-tempered and still-wet crowd didn't have a lot of patience for the guys on the undercard. And the Florida tag team title match with a screw-job ending pissed them off even more.

The only time they seemed to perk up at all was for Firefly, a female wrestler, and a real acrobat. She'd graduated from Florida State's Flying High Circus up in Tallahassee. Athletic and toned, she could, as the old song went, "fly through the air with the greatest of ease." Ernie saw her potential, but as tough as this business could be for the guys it was that much harder for the women. And Ernie had a hard time finding legitimate enough competition for Firefly to really put her over with the fans.

For Gorpp's first opponent, Ernie picked a popular midcarder he'd brought in before from up in the Georgia territory. "Mr. America," Mark Carter, had been a Navy SEAL before he got a dishonorable discharge. But Ernie had gotten him over before as a babyface (what wrestlers called the good guys) doing a kind of Captain America homage when fans were susceptible to feeling particularly xenophobic. In the past, Ernie had put him up against "commies" and foreigners who were billed as being from the mystic Orient, the jungles of Africa, or often just from parts unknown.

Ernie thought Mr. America would be the right foil to insert into the storyline about an invader from another world. And he'd come up with the perfect ring walk music for Gorpp the Grappler.

In 1957, Billy Lee Riley and his Little Green Men had what some called a novelty hit—but a hit nonetheless—on Sun Records with "Flying Saucers Rock-n-Roll." As soon as the song started, they turned the house lights up and all eyes turned to the heels' (villains') locker room entrance which led to the ring. For a few long moments there was nothing to see, but then the curtain parted and Gorpp appeared with his eggshell suit, his giant head and his black almond eyes. He had no robe, no towel, no manager and no valet. He stood alone in the entryway and a hush spread across the Armory.

The next thing Gorpp knew, Levey was saying, "hailing from parts unknown, Gorpp the Grappler!" The crowd booed and worse. A couple people even hurled their half full beer cans at Gorpp, but with terrible aim. Ernie knew his crowd and they didn't want any freak-headed foreigner taking over their territory. They were behind Mr. America all the way. Some were even waving American flags in the bleachers.

Ernie made sure the camera guy got a shot of that.

Most matches were works, meaning the result had been predetermined and some of the moves may have been worked out ahead of time or at least worked out in the ring. But Ernie told Carter this would be a shoot, meaning he and Gorpp were going to give it their best shot, and may the best man win.

Shoots were rare by the 1970s but kayfabe was still very much in effect, meaning for anyone in the wrestling business that to let on the matches were works would be breaking the cardinal rule. Rule Number One in professional wrestling.

Carter could sell as a babyface but, like most guys in this line of work, he was another tough sumbitch. He didn't mind a good old fashioned shoot.

Ernie didn't talk about it either way with Gorpp. The more time he spent with him the harder it got to figure out how to really get through to him. Ernie worried that trying to smarten him up would just confuse matters. He wanted this Gorpp angle to work out. Ernie thought he could be a real draw, but he also didn't mind rolling the dice and seeing how things played out.

That turned out to be too bad for Mark Carter.

Gorpp showed patience and let Carter try to be the aggressor early on. At one point, the crowd even got to cheer when Carter got Gorpp turned around and put him in a full nelson. But, he couldn't hold on to him, and when he made the mistake of turning his back, just for a second, Gorpp got him in the already pre-sold flying saucer. The crowd had been sufficiently awed just by Gorpp's appearance when he emerged from behind the curtain. But, when 2,500 soaking wet wrestling fans saw Gorpp turn himself and Mr. America into a spinning blur, then Carter crashing into the crowd in the eighteenth row, an old lady's dentures popping out and Carter breaking an ankle and two ribs, a legend was born.

The referee counted Carter out and raised Gorpp's hand in victory. Levey stepped back into the ring and announced Gorpp the winner as Ernie sent a stretcher out to bring Carter back to the babyface dressing room. In a rare misstep, Ernie didn't coordinate with Levey about the after match interview, perhaps because of how unusual it was not to know ahead of time who the winner would be. Out of force of habit, Levey asked Gorpp if he had a message for the fans there at the Bayfront Armory, then he put the microphone close enough for Gorpp to speak into it.

To Ernie's surprise, he did.

"I am Gorpp. I am here on Earth to defeat your World Champion." The Armory got very quiet. Gorpp looked around, then left the ring and made the walk back down the aisle to the locker room. They were still getting Carter loaded up on the stretcher. Ernie followed Gorpp. He needed to have a word with his new featured attraction, but when he pushed the curtain back and went into the heels' locker room there was no sign of him.

CHAPTER 8

On Monday, Gorpp showed up at his regularly scheduled training time, but Ernie had told Bobby and the boys to hang back until later. He needed some one-on-one time with Gorpp. When he saw Gorpp emerge through the curtain he stepped out of his office and waved him in with a plume of smoke from his cigarette. Gorpp followed and sat down, as little scraps of paper and old cigarette butts were pushed across the promoter's desk by the oscillating fan.

Ernie swiveled his creaky old chair around and rubbed his hands up and down his thighs a couple times, a nervous tic. "Well, son, that was quite a show. You got way over. That's for sure." Ernie grabbed an envelope off his desk and handed it to Gorpp. "There's your pay. And there's more where that came from if we can keep this going. You want to keep it going?"

"I want to defeat the World Champion," Gorpp said.

"Well, we get a few more headlines like this one and a title shot just may be in the cards." Ernie handed Gorpp a copy of the *Tampa Times*. There was a picture of Gorpp speaking into Steve Levey's microphone and a smaller shot of Mark Carter on a stretcher. The headline on the front page read:

ALIEN INVASION AT THE BAYFRONT ARMORY?

Below that was a picture and side story about Tampa residents claiming to see those strange lights, and now wrestling fans were claiming to have seen an actual alien. Neither the money nor the newspaper interested Gorpp. He set them both down on a teetering stack of file folders and returned his attention to Ernie.

"Listen, son. There's a talk we need to have if we're gonna get all we can out of this schtick. Have you ever heard of kayfabe?"

Gorpp didn't respond.

"What it means is a magician never tells you how he does his tricks, right?"

Still no response.

"For us, in the wrestling biz, it means we don't never reveal how we do *our* tricks, understand? You, me, your opponent and the referee, we're the only ones who need to know how a match is gonna go. We don't talk about it to our wives or girlfriends. We don't cry home to our mommies when we gotta do a job. Not our best friend. Not the press. No one."

Ernie kept going for a while but Gorpp tuned out before long. Nothing Ernie said made much sense to him, and Ernie soon realized not only that he wasn't getting through to Gorpp about kayfabe, but that he couldn't imagine this guy having a mom or girlfriend. He couldn't rightly imagine where Gorpp had come from, and sitting this close to him was starting to give him the willies. And Ernie started to realize the whole idea of deception or lying, or working a match, was a completely foreign concept to Gorpp, perhaps one he would have trouble grasping. If that was true, to get the most out of his run, he'd just have to keep winning shoots.

CHAPTER 9

Gorpp had covered his vessel with some old tarps he found on the roof of the Ambassador, but now he fortified the camouflage in preparation for a road trip. Heavyweight Championship Wrestling from Florida was taking their new featured attraction on a statewide tour, and Gorpp came to understand he would be traveling with the boys.

Ernie wanted to keep an eye on him.

They would start the next day in Sarasota, then go to Ft. Myers, over to Miami, up to West Palm, then Orlando and wrap up in Jacksonville and Tallahassee. Ernie told the boys if the 'seven cards in seven cities in seven days' tour was a success, they'd take a couple days off at Panama City Beach. But the truth was, with his strange new star attraction and no worked matches, Ernie didn't have a clue what was going to happen.

One thing that did happen, which no one would have predicted, was that Gorpp quickly became the designated driver. Ernie, Levey and the boys in the locker room all liked to get pretty hammered most every road trip. Sometimes after the matches. Sometimes before. And often with two hundred or more miles to drive to get home after the shows. Gorpp didn't drink. No one ever saw him get tired. And he seemed a little claustrophobic and on edge as a passenger in Ernie's old van. Driving gave him something to do, and that seemed like a good thing. The guys got a kick out of the looks he'd get from other drivers, especially kids in the backseat. Ernie had a hunch Gorpp had never driven before, but he just seemed to take to it, intuitively.

They wrestled outside under a big yellow moon at the Sarasota Amphitheater. It was foggy, humid and not too hot for midsummer. They got a bit of breeze off the Gulf. The PA sounded pretty rinky-dink with the wind blowing, but it still struck a chord with this new crowd who'd only heard rumors, if anything, about Gorpp the Grappler. But, just like in Tampa, the moment he came into view and just stood stoic, facing the crowd, he was over. His opponent was a hometown hero, a former surfer who still projected that image with his tan, tie-dye trunks and signature surf board he carried with him to the ring. Wade "Big Wave" Rich.

Wade cut a promo that aired on the last week's program from Bayfront saying he'd never met a man from our world, or any other, who was stronger than a wave, or more cunning. "I don't care where he's from," Wade said, with a stern expression and a finger pointing at the camera. "What I care about is where he's going, because that's down, brother! Down on the mat where I'll ride him like my surfboard. Oh yeah!" That was Wade's signature move, he'd get a guy face down on the mat then climb on his back and ride him like a surfboard, pressing his organs into the canvass until he conceded.

It didn't usually take long.

But tonight, wrestling fans would be treated to that rare wrestling unicorn, the shoot. Ernie pulled Wade aside into a cloud of cigarette smoke in the roped off area behind the amphitheater.

"Listen, Wade. We've made some money together over the

years and we're gonna make some money tonight, but I just want *you* to know that *I* don't know what my guy's gonna do out there."

"Don't patronize me, Mr. Cantrell. This ain't my first rodeo. I been in the mix plenty of times."

"I appreciate that, Wade. What I'm telling you is this is something different."

Ernie's talk didn't have the effect of spooking Wade Rich. If anything, he had even less respect for Gorpp going into the match than he would have had otherwise. After some intensive training and a real match under his belt, Gorpp was improving. In under five minutes, he had Wade in the flying saucer. When his flailing limbs came into clear sight after the blur of the flying saucer, Wade landed hard on the concrete steps and hit the aluminum handrail hard enough to crack his shin bone.

The storyline in the wrestling and mainstream news media focused on the unknown origins of this new wrestling phenomenon, and also the fact his opponents were being carried off on stretchers.

The Ft. Myers match the next night was cancelled at the last minute. We now know the hometown favorite there, Rich Robbie Sanborn, the "Naples Playboy," also ran the territory. No one knew it at the time, but the suspension placed on Sanborn was all him weaving his own web. He suspended himself to get out of wrestling this unearthly menace that crazy old Ernie Cantrell had loosed on the Florida territory.

Miami was on in a big way. Ernie had a Seminole Indian down there who came from the swamps of the Everglades and was over with both the whites and the Latinos in Miami. John White Eagle was the name bestowed on him by Ernie Cantrell. John was a natural athlete. Quick. Graceful. He could work a convincing match with no hard bumps. The older guys really liked working with him because he made them look good. When it came to the business, John was wise beyond his years. And he was the only one to give Ernie grief about a shoot.

Ernie didn't like talking on the phone, especially when he hadn't initiated the call. But when John White Eagle called him at his hotel on the day of the cancelled Ft. Myers show, Ernie knew he had to talk to him.

"Hello, Mr. Cantrell. Thank you for taking my call. I just—"

"Cut to the chase, Johnny. I ain't got time for chit chat."

"Ok. Who is this guy, and why did I get a call from Bobby telling me I'm shooting with this freak that's sending guys to the hospital?"

"I've always been straight with you, Johnny. And I'm gonna be straight with you now. I don't know. I'll be damned if I can figure this guy out. I know we can all make a lot of money with him, but I don't know what he's gonna do. I can't connect with him. I can't come to an understanding with the guy so I can smarten him up. That's all I can tell you. Get ready for a big payday if you don't back out like Robbie Sanborn. Fucking guy found a way to weasel out and he missed a payday. So that's it, Johnny. What's it gonna be? You in or you out?"

John White Eagle thought about it. If they sold out the Hollywood Wrestletorium he could make a down payment on that catamaran he'd been eyeing.

"I'm in."

CHAPTER 10

It wasn't just a sellout. They were turning them away. Firefly had a tough go with the "Puerto Rican Princess" Mia Camila. The crowd was a mix of Cubans, Seminoles and whites from as far away as the Treasure Coast. This time, as soon as Gorpp emerged, he got booed. He didn't show it, but it surprised him. They weren't awed by him in Miami.

They were squarely against him.

He made his ring walk to a hail of popcorn boxes, empty beer cans and even a lit cigar. He paid little attention and suffered no grave injuries.

When Levey announced John White Eagle, the place erupted. True to his custom, White Eagle bounded to the ring barefoot. He hopped over the top rope and quickly ran by Gorpp slapping him on the chest as he passed. The crowd ate it up.

Gorpp didn't respond.

Once they got down to business, both realized this would be perhaps their most difficult match to date. White Eagle's speed meant Gorpp couldn't predict his movements. They both spent enough time circling and sizing up their opponent that the crowd got restless. When they tangled it looked like a dog fight. The eruptions were violent and so fast you couldn't tell who was getting the best of it. Then they would break. After one such clash, White Eagle came away with a big gash across his cheek. He couldn't continue. The result was recorded as a forfeit by White Eagle. He got paid. And he got thirty-six stitches in his cheek. As one sports writer noted, at least he avoided being hurled like a projectile into the stands.

As Gorpp's reign of terror continued into the Florida panhandle, the storylines shifted to it being miraculous his opponents weren't getting more severely injured. One reporter with the *Jacksonville Daily Record* tried to call Ernie Cantrell for a comment. But Ernie never returned his call.

Between the mainstream media coverage of UFOs and the scandals around Gorpp sending his opponents to the hospital, the Florida shoot tour was an unmitigated success, even with the last minute cancellation in Naples. Ernie didn't lose any sleep over a broken collarbone or a couple cracked ribs. These were big boys who took the payday and knew what they were getting into.

His main concern at that point was Gorpp's star rising, shining and burning out too quickly. Usually, if you were lucky, you got either the great gimmick or the guy who could really wrestle. Gorpp was both rolled into one. And he was so spooky looking he didn't need to do promos or even interviews. It turned out to be better that he didn't. Added to the mystique. His face got plastered on the cover of wrestling magazines, Florida newspapers and the tabloids too.

And every show sold out.

Speculation in the wrestling magazines turned to a world title shot. That didn't help Ernie. He needed time to tease the story out. This was all going too fast. He decided to do something that hadn't occurred to Gorpp. He sidelined him. He had other guys he wanted to keep in front of fans and he needed to let the "invader from another world" storyline cool off a bit so he could bring it back and keep milking it. As soon as he told the guys in the locker room, and Gorpp, the problems started.

Gorpp wasn't happy about it. He said something about needing his chance to challenge for the world title as soon as possible, but Ernie tuned him out.

That's what they all said.

The other guys weren't happy, because even though they were getting a chance at the spotlight, the crowds weren't showing up, and since their takes represented a percentage of the door, they were losing money.

The tabloids starting running stories saying the alien had returned to his home world.

That's when the real problems started.

CHAPTER 11

Earl Kruddup, Jr. ran Heavyweight Championship Wrestling of the Southeast, a territory that included parts of Louisiana, Mississippi, Alabama, Georgia and even northwest Florida. For all those years when Kruddup, Sr. ran Southeast, he and Ernie had an understanding. They didn't encroach on each other's territories. But, now that Junior had taken over, all bets were off. He had been promoting matches in Pensacola for two years now, and rumor had it he was in talks with a concern in Bay County about matches there too.

Junior's latest insult wasn't original by any means, but it was, as far as Ernie Cantrell was concerned, below the belt. When Ernie went dark with Gorpp's storyline, Junior decided to fill the void with his own "invader from another world" routine. His knockoff was an over the hill mid-lister with an alien mask who, unable to do even a bad imitation of the flying saucer, instead had green mist he used to supposedly paralyze his opponents. Junior may have pocketed a few extra bucks on the first couple outings for his imposter but word quickly spread this knockoff was more than *a little green* when it came to selling the whole 'being from another world' routine.

With assurances that his hiatus would only be temporary, Gorpp continued showing up for training with Bobby and Ernie. Ernie felt it was important to keep in regular touch with Gorpp. He still hadn't been able to get a home address or phone number out of him. And that day in his office, he'd left the envelope of money Ernie gave him just sitting there. Ernie hadn't offered to pay him since and Gorpp never brought it up.

That was definitely a first.

When Ernie thought about it, he realized he'd never seen Gorpp eat, take a shit or make a phone call. It was just weird. He tried not to think about it.

The day after Gorpp learned about Kruddup, Jr.'s imposter he didn't show up for training with Bobby. Bobby immediately alerted Ernie, but with no way to contact Gorpp, there wasn't anything they could do about it. A couple days later, Ernie got an unexpected call from Junior. Against his better instincts, he took it.

"Mr. Cantrell?" Junior's voice cracked. He didn't usually show the respect of calling him "Mr. Cantrell."

"Junior? You sound like you seen a ghost, son."

"Mr. Cantrell, I just, well, I didn't know who else to call. I guess maybe I need to call the law. I don't know."

Ernie flashed on Gorpp's disappearance but didn't want to jump to conclusions. "Tell me what you seen, Junior."

"Well, Mr. Cantrell. Buddy Graham, you know Buddy. He's been with me since, well, since when my dad was still alive. He came on with my dad."

"I remember Buddy." Buddy Graham had actually started out with Ernie and then moved on to a series of territories. Kruddup's would be the last in a long line.

"Right. Well, he's the one been doing the, well the 'little green man' schtick. I don't know if you'd heard."

"I heard." It turned Ernie's stomach to think of a mid-card

wrestler like Buddy Graham, now in his fifties, trying to sell the Gorpp routine.

"Well, it's just business, right?"

Ernie didn't dignify Junior's bullshit with a response. He just kept thinking to himself that Junior was the one who was a little green.

"Anyway, Buddy didn't show up for a house show yesterday in Mobile. And that's just not like him. So, I called his old lady. Or common law wife, whatever you call it. They been shacked up since Buddy got back from—"

"Get to the point, Junior."

"Mr. Cantrell, Sue was so upset on the phone I couldn't make heads or tails of what she was trying to tell me. I drove out to their place and knocked on the door. I saw her looking through the blinds but she wouldn't answer. She saw something, Mr. Cantrell. Something that scared the hell out of her. I think at one point she said, 'It was him. It was him.' I just didn't know who else to call."

Ernie watched the slips of paper on his desk lift up when the fan turned toward him, then fall back down when it swung back. He coughed a couple times.

"Mr. Cantrell? I just didn't know who else to call."

CHAPTER 12

THE NEXT MORNING, Gorpp reported right on time for his session with Bobby. He didn't volunteer any information about where he'd been. He didn't look or act any different. There were no bloodstains on his eggshell white trunks and boots. Ernie decided nothing good could come from asking questions, so Bobby got Gorpp back doing ringwork with some of the boys.

CHAPTER 13

HOWIE SHOWS, the longtime editor of *World Wrestling Digest*, got Ernie to agree to an interview with Gorpp under two conditions: that Ernie would be present, and that he would have final sign-off on the copy before they went to print.

Howie flew in to Tampa from JFK, rented a car and went straight to the Armory where Bobby was working with Gorpp. He stood in the back and just watched him for a while. Ernie ambled over to join him.

"You haven't seen him in person yet, have you?"

"No, no," Howie said. He pulled a pencil out from behind his ear and scratched his crazy Einstein poof of hair. "Where'd you find this guy, Ernie?"

"I thought you wanted to talk to him," Ernie said.

"Yeah, yeah," Howie answered, like he was snapping out of a deep thought. "Let's do it."

They walked together slowly toward the ring as if Gorpp were a wild animal. And maybe he was.

Ernie reached up and held on to the lower ring rope. "Bobby, take a break, eh? Son," he said to Gorpp, "come down here. Someone I'd like you to meet."

Gorpp dutifully hopped down out of the ring and stood before Howie.

"Hi, Gorpp," Howie said extending a hand. "What's your real name anyway?" He pulled a pad from his back pocket.

Gorpp didn't extend a hand in return or answer his question. Ernie couldn't help but smirk. He knew the feeling.

Howie shot a look at Ernie.

"Listen, son," Ernie said to Gorpp, "this here is Howard Shows. More people read what he writes about professional wrestling than anyone else. If Howie here goes back up to New York City and writes a big piece about you in his magazine, it can only help move you closer to that title shot."

Gorpp fixed his gaze on Shows. "I am Gorpp," he said.

Howie cupped his hands over his ears, almost stabbing himself with his pencil in the process. He took a few steps back from Gorpp.

"Where you from, uh, Gorpp?"

Gorpp verbalized something but it just caused Shows and Ernie to cringe, cover their ears and step even further back. Gorpp was still learning how to modulate his voice to be less abrasive to human ears. And it wouldn't be until later that Gorpp would learn the Earth word for his home world, a moon orbiting Saturn that we call Enceladus.

"What are your goals here?" Howie soldiered on.

"I want to challenge the World Champion. My goal is to take over the planet Earth."

"Right, sure. Say, where did you learn that flying saucer move you do? You get some real speed with that thing."

Gorpp didn't respond.

"This may sound like a strange question, but are you human, son?"

"I am Gorpp."

CHAPTER 14

AFTER HOWIE'S COVER STORY, the *New York Post* ran a sensational story of their own that collected bits from all the regional and wrestling coverage of Gorpp. Then the call came. The promoter for Madison Square Garden wanted to host a rematch between Gorpp and John White Eagle.

This was the big time.

Ernie sold Gorpp on the match as a stepping stone to the World Championship. And since Gorpp showed no interest in getting paid, Ernie was able to sweeten the pot for the reticent and recently maimed White Eagle by offering him part of Gorpp's purse. It worked, and the match was set. Ernie pocketed the rest of Gorpp's take.

It was billed as "a match from out of this world." Howie's *World Wrestling Digest* and other wrestling magazines splashed pictures of White Eagle's gashed cheek on their covers with smaller shots of ambulances loading up the likes of Mark Carter and some of Gorpp's other conquests.

Gorpp hadn't wrestled a dozen times and he was headlining a sold out show at the Garden. He was a prodigy and an oddity. Most importantly, he sold tickets.

Lots of tickets.

CHAPTER 15

THE GARDEN HAD ONCE BEEN the premiere address for bigtime professional wrestling. From Ed "Strangler" Lewis to Jim Londos. From Lou Thesz to Bruno Sammartino.

Ernie bought Gorpp a plane ticket, though he wondered if he even had any ID. As it turned out, Gorpp said he would provide his own transportation. Ernie worried Gorpp would be a no show and there would be hell to pay with the national office, not to mention the Garden promoter.

He needn't have worried.

To Gorpp, the trip to New York was akin to moving your car to the parking space across the street. He found an old warehouse near the Garden where he could stow his vessel, then made his way on foot to the venue. Fans started to notice him almost as soon as he scaled down the warehouse wall to the street. They called out to him but didn't dare approach and he paid them no mind.

What Gorpp didn't know was that a radar had flagged him going off course and within a few minutes (to them) Central Command had dispatched a patrol to find out what had happened to Gorpp. When the patrol arrived where

Gorpp had been keeping his vessel on the roof of the Ambassador Hotel in Tampa, he'd just left for New York. The patrol, of course, immediately picked up the new location on his sensors, but then he got called back for a more pressing matter. It would be months in Earth time before they got around to looking for him again.

Gorpp felt none of the nostalgia or sense of reverence for the venue that so many wrestling fans, and people who worked in the business, felt upon entering those hallowed halls at Madison Square Garden. Gorpp found it to be larger and a little cleaner than the Bayfront Armory, but not much. He had little interest in the proceedings other than as a necessary stepping stone to get to the World Championship.

Their match started out much as it had in Miami but without the slap on the chest before the bell rang this time. Both were wary of one another, and both were even more cautious than before. There weren't the violent tangles of last time that left White Eagle with a gash on his cheek and a mandatory forfeit.

At almost the thirty-minute mark of a match scheduled for sixty minutes, Gorpp got White Eagle up on his shoulders for the flying saucer. Oddly, it seemed White Eagle didn't resist and it also looked like he'd managed to hook his arms through Gorpp's in a way none of Gorpp's previous victims had. Gorpp got up to speed so that he was just a blur, like a spinning top with White Eagle whirring above his head. What happened this time though was that when Gorpp attempted to let White Eagle loose, his arm had become locked together with White Eagle's. When White Eagle went flying out of the ring, Gorpp was tied up with him and they sailed out together, a mass of tangled limbs. They crashed into the announcers' table, breaking it in half, and both were counted out by the referee, so the bout ended up a draw.

Insiders thought it had all the telltale signs of a work.

Neither lost face. The New York fans and press got a show, and there was still reason for a third contest between the two. As it turned out, this was all just serendipity, since this match, like all of Gorpp's matches to that point, had been a straight shoot.

CHAPTER 16

When Howie's new issue came out, Gorpp was ranked as the number one challenger for Black Jack Tolliver's title, and John White Eagle was ranked number two. After a conversation between Tolliver, Heavyweight Championship Wrestling's national president, Sam Calvin, and Ernie, Calvin announced there would be a no holds barred, no count outs, and no time limit third match between Gorpp the Grappler and John White Eagle. And the winner would meet Tolliver for a shot at the title before the year was out.

The third and final match took place in the Orange Bowl in Little Havana, where the Superbowl had been played several times before. Almost overnight, Gorpp had risen to superstar status. The match fell just short of selling out the Orange Bowl where the capacity was north of 75,000.

Sam Calvin and Ernie Cantrell made the most of this Superbowl of professional wrestling. They had a long undercard, tributes to fallen heroes and more pageantry and hoopla than either really felt comfortable with, but hey, it sold tickets and spoke to the significance of the event. Firefly was disappointed not to be included on the Madison Square Garden card, but here in Florida Ernie called the shots, and she got a good placement.

Celebrities were spotted throughout the crowd from Muhammed Ali to Jack Nicholson and, most importantly to wrestling fans, the World Champion, Black Jack Tolliver sat at ringside. Like Firefly, Steve Levey was disappointed he couldn't make the Madison Square Garden trip, but here in Florida, he set the scene as dusk settled over the Orange Bowl and the hours counted down to the main event. Tolliver joined Levey for a short interview during the final intermission.

Levey asked the Champion if he'd ever seen anything like Gorpp the Grappler. Tolliver made light of the phenomenon Gorpp had become. "There's always a new kid on the block with a new gimmick, a new fad. These things come and go. I've stood the test of time and I'll stand the test against whichever of these boys wins here tonight."

Levey started to ask Tolliver what the largest crowd was he'd ever wrestled in front of, knowing it wouldn't come close to this. Tolliver gave him a nasty look and beat a hasty retreat from the hot microphone, returning to his entourage at ringside.

After all the buildup, the third and final match between Gorpp and White Eagle seemed to be over before it began. This time, as soon as the bell rang, they clenched and within a minute Gorpp had White Eagle in some sort of submission hold and he tapped out almost immediately. Gorpp's hand was raised in victory. Levey looked over to Tolliver's seat to see if he could wave the champ over for a post-match comment, but the champ was gone.

CHAPTER 17

Gorpp would have welcomed the match with Tolliver as soon as White Eagle conceded, but he learned soon enough that's not the way it works. To properly monetize the super event, promoters and magazine publishers, television stations and sponsors needed time to build up to it. This was all an interminable bore to Gorpp, and he worried more with each passing Earth day that he would be called back to answer for his absence and insubordination before he had a chance to prove himself here among the enemy.

Then, to make matters worse, as the match drew near, Tolliver shocked the wrestling world by announcing his retirement. Consensus was he'd rather go out on top, and with no broken bones or the humiliation of tapping out to mysterious submission holds; that to keep his ego intact, he would forfeit the title and forego the big payday. Ernie wondered if it would have made any difference if he'd offered him part of Gorpp's purse, as he'd done to entice White Eagle into the Madison Square Garden affair. After seeing the same performance Tolliver saw at the Orange Bowl, he tended to doubt it.

With the title now vacant and Gorpp already promised a

shot at it, it was decided there would be a tournament to determine who Gorpp would face for the crown. Notably, none of Gorpp's former opponents, including White Eagle, entered the tournament.

"Iron Claw" Martinez came out of retirement in San Juan to enter the contest. Some young prospects like "The Russian Blackbird," Dimitri Drozdov and "Lightning" Jackson from Dallas stepped up too. Gorpp had no interest in the tournament, which he saw as just more minutiae and delay that wasted precious time.

Precious and perishable time.

CHAPTER 18

Dimitri Drozdov had been something of a sensation in Mother Russia, even though he won the gold medal as an amateur in the 1968 Olympics in Mexico for the American team. He grew up in Alaska. He turned pro in Europe shortly after the Olympics, but he'd only recently started wrestling in the lower forty-eight.

Like Gorpp's flying saucer, Drozdov had his own signature, but it wasn't really a move or a hold. It was Drozdov's stare. It came to be known as the deadlights. In his matches, when an opponent did something that really angered the Russian, he would fix a deathlike stare on them before exploding with an attack that few had been able to repel.

After a four-week-long elimination tournament, the final match took place at Olympic Auditorium in Los Angeles. The final two contestants were Drozdov and the "Ugandan Giant," Makusa. The tournament had done good business, and now that it came down to two, speculation returned to Gorpp and if anyone could stop him.

For the first part of the match it appeared Makusa would be too much for Drozdov. About twenty minutes in, he lifted Drozdov up over his head, as if he would do an airplane spin, perhaps he intended it as a message to Gorpp. But instead, he just hurled Drozdov over the top rope. The referee started counting and the dazed Drozdov put his fingers on the ring apron to pull himself up. Before he could, Makusa stomped on his hand, causing Drozdov to fall back to the floor grasping his fingers in agony. The ref warned Makusa and started the count anew. Drozdov reached his trembling fingers back up to the ring apron, and as the referee counted "seven… eight…" Makusa stomped even harder on Drozdov's already injured hand. But this time, instead of falling back down to the floor, he kept pulling himself up. The referee tried to warn Makusa again, but the Giant shoved him aside and brought his big boot down again on Drozdov's hand. The Russian didn't move it. Didn't respond at all other than to train his death stare—the deadlights—on Makusa.

As he started his climb, the Giant backed up. Once in the ring, the crowd rose up in support of the Russian Blackbird and he flew toward Makusa in an explosion of violence that culminated in the smaller man raising the Giant over his own head. You could see the blood pulsing in his neck and arm veins as he held the Ugandan Giant above his head and then hurled *him* over the top rope and out of the ring. The referee started counting, but it was clear to ringside observers that Makusa wanted no more of being in the ring with Dimitri Drozdov whose hand, crushed fingers and all, was raised as the winner of the tournament and the one chosen to face Gorpp the Grappler for the World Heavyweight Championship.

CHAPTER 19

Two important things had begun to dawn on Gorpp.

The first was that Dimitri Drozdov posed no real threat to him. The World Championship was as good as his, as soon as he could actually find his way into the ring to compete for it. But the second thing was, at some indiscernible moment, he realized he had conflated some sort of construct or symbology, again, alien to him, with the actual overthrow of Earth.

One of the failures of Gorpp's training for the invasion had been, with so little left to chance, he had woefully little reason to employ critical or creative thinking. It was all paint-by-numbers, and that led to cognitive atrophy.

Now, thrust into such a primitive and altogether alien culture, he found that even as a lesser among his own, he had found a way to live as a great achiever among Earthlings. But, he also had to give weight to his complete failure to recognize that the World Championship had no real worth. His kind were so unaccustomed to imagination, storytelling, myth or deceit that naiveté allowed him to accept at face value something with another meaning entirely.

He found his mind drifting, as it often did. But this time,

into a more existential quandary. Of a kind he was altogether unfamiliar with considering.

Gorpp didn't question politically, philosophically or even intellectually, his mission, his orders, or his duties. He had simply become viscerally intolerant of the tedium. But, now he had broken Rule Number One and was out cavorting with the natives—experiencing the syrupy slow Earth time and metabolism, smelling the sweat of Earthlings, hearing them scream with joy and anguish during the matches—he started to see his life in a different light. Maybe he *should* question his mission and the life that had been chosen for him. Maybe he was right to think he could win the Championship, but maybe he was wrong that it didn't matter. Just because it didn't matter to his kind, so what? It sure mattered to Earthlings. He could live like a king as the World Champion on Earth, even if it didn't mean what he had thought. It could still mean respect and celebrity, status and privilege, here on Earth.

Gorpp had the revelation that he wanted to reign, not *over* Earth, but *on* Earth as the World Heavyweight Champion. He would face this "Russian Blackbird," Dimitri Drozdov, and his deadlights, and he would prevail.

CHAPTER 20

GORPP AND DROZDOV squared off at the Omni in Atlanta with the vacant World Heavyweight Championship on the line.

Drozdov was rugged, well trained and determined, and he could relate strongly with Gorpp's original motivations to bring the World Championship back to his people. And, he was almost surely doping. He would represent Gorpp's first real test and again, Ernie Cantrell couldn't have scripted a worked storyline any better.

It was all coming up aces for Ernie in '75.

The Russian heel entered to the national anthem of the Union of Soviet Socialist Republics.

"Unbreakable Union of freeborn Republics, great Russia has welded forever to stand. Created in struggle by will of the people, united and mighty, our Soviet land!"

As planned, it drew heat in Atlanta, Georgia.

Meanwhile, in less than a year, Gorpp the Grappler had gone from the mysterious heel we were all afraid of, to a rock star we all wanted a ticket to see. Now, instead of facing off as the outsider against Mr. America, Gorpp was America personified. He was a spectacle and a renegade, and a winner with a good gimmick.

What could be more American than that?

Now, instead of going up against Mr. America, Ernie and Sam Calvin set it up so Gorpp would face Mr. USSR, Dimitri Drozdov.

Later, some said Gorpp had looked past Dimitri, that he didn't take him seriously enough, didn't fully appreciate his amateur background, his almost desperate motivation. And the deadlights. All of that was probably true but it still wouldn't have been enough if Dimitri and his trainer hadn't devised a brilliant strategy.

The strategy was to disable Gorpp's right rotator cuff so he couldn't lift Dimitri up for the flying saucer. As soon as the bell rang, Dimitri leapt like the Russian Blackbird and delivered a perfectly placed chop straight down into Gorpp's shoulder joint. The pain was unlike anything Gorpp had experienced in or out of the ring. He was pulled violently into his meditative space but the fireworks of pain exploding out from his shoulder followed him, even there. He lost his balance, fell to one knee and left himself completely exposed so Dimitri delivered another, even more savage chop to the same exact spot. Gorpp crumpled in pain and started emitting a kind of rhythmic shriek that caused the packed crowd at the Omni to hold their hands over their ears. They said it was a god-awful thing to hear, that much pain.

Gorpp lay in a fetal position, rocking back and forth on the mat, holding his shoulder with his good arm until the sounds started to fade. It seemed almost as if he were going to sleep. That's when Dimitri started in kicking and stomping on Gorpp's injured shoulder. It was the kind of angle Ernie had orchestrated many times.

But this wasn't an angle.

This was real, and Ernie started to worry Dimitri would do permanent damage to Gorpp's shoulder. That's when the clicking, squealing sounds stopped. Gorpp raised his head to look into Dimitri's eyes and you would think the deadlights were Gorpp's signature. His black, almond eyes locked onto Dimitri's like damnation itself. Dimitri wasn't one to back down from anyone, but even while Gorpp was still on hands and knees, once their eyes met, Dimitri put his hands up, as if to ward off an evil spirit, and started backing away.

Dimitri got as far as the ring ropes, but as he made the same mistake Bobby had—of turning his back to Gorpp to go through them—he was attacked from behind. Before he could react, the dreaded outcome he'd trained for and prepared to avoid started happening. Somehow, Gorpp had him up on his shoulders, even with what must surely be ripped ligaments and tendons in his rotator cuff, if not shattered bones. He trembled in pain but somehow managed to get Dimitri spinning in the dreaded flying saucer. But when he tried to hurl the Russian into the crowd, his shoulder gave out. Dimitri still went over the top rope but only flew far enough to land in a heap on the laps of a group of youngsters from a nearby children's hospital. Fortunately, the only real injury came when Dimitri's elbow busted open the lip of a ten-year-old boy in the front row. The boy couldn't have been more proud.

Gorpp had no way of knowing where Dimitri would land, especially with his injured shoulder. He had no idea the children from the hospital were going to be there. And he certainly had no idea that Dimitri's teenaged nephew was in intensive care after a hunting accident where their family lived in Nikolaevsk, Alaska. Gorpp didn't use the term "bullshit," but if he had, that's what he would have thought of Dimitri's deadlights signature. To Gorpp, the idea of being paralyzed by fear was as foreign as lying or monetary currency. What he learned that night in the Omni was that he'd never been stared at in the same way Dimitri did when he extricated himself from those children, and their crutches and wheelchairs and oxygen tanks.

The referee started counting and Dimitri started marching toward the ring. He hoisted himself up on the apron at seven and climbed through the ropes at nine, never taking his eyes off Gorpp.

The final act of their improvised masterpiece looked like a clinic in the science of wrestling. You could easily have mistaken it for a finals match in the Olympics. Each had the upper hand at different times but neither could assert his will over the other.

They were both too good.

Gorpp had Dimitri in a front face lock when he pulled one arm up over his head. He was straining again and in obvious pain from his shoulder. With one final gasp of resolve, Gorpp hooked Dimitri's far leg with his opposite leg, grabbed Dimitri's other leg with his hand and rolled him up into what's called an inside cradle, or small package. Dimitri kicked desperately but couldn't free himself before the referee counted three.

The picture on the cover of *World Wrestling Digest* showed the referee raising Gorpp's hand before he handed him the belt. Gorpp was on his knees, clearly exhausted and still wincing in pain. In the background, Dimitri could be seen, still on his back with his hands over his face.

A once in a lifetime opportunity, squandered.

Dimitri's trainer and handler, Alexi Ivanof, actually filed a complaint with Heavyweight Championship Wrestling and the Georgia Athletic Commission, saying that Gorpp should have been ineligible to even compete because he had never produced any identification. Dimitri got hassled over his paperwork constantly, and he was an American citizen! The complaint even went so far as to suggest Gorpp wasn't from Earth. Sam Calvin, Ernie Cantrell and their good friends at the Athletic Commission were all enjoying huge profits, sellout crowds and an endless parade of headlines with Gorpp the Grappler. They weren't about to mess that up just to placate a couple of Russkies.

CHAPTER 21

AFTER SURVIVING the deadlights and nursing his shoulder a bit, Gorpp loosened up a little and started enjoying being Champion. He handled his own travel and never once asked for a penny in payment. Not for plane tickets or gas or hotels or per diem. None of it. So, not only did Ernie and Sam Calvin have their biggest star ever, they were making money hand over fist and pocketing it all. It was too good to be true. Gorpp even started selling for his opponents occasionally. It was considered the greatest honor in wrestling to be put over by the champ.

He did a Broadway (where a match ends in a time limit draw) with the Masked Destroyer in Charlotte that made headlines. His cage match with "Chainsaw" Charlie Carver served as a tribute to one of wrestling's most reliable workers for forty years, but Gorpp had to carry the over-the-hill Carver to make it watchable. There was even a rumor he wrestled Dusty Rhodes to a double disqualification in a Texas Chain Match in Amarillo, but strangely, there's no record of it.

CHAPTER 22

Ernie was headed to his room in a hotel in San Diego. That afternoon, Gorpp had a meet-and-greet with fans to sign pictures of him doing the flying saucer with Ed Wood-style UFOs in the sky above. That night he had a match with the California State Champion at the San Diego Civic Center. Ernie looked down over the rail and a buxom blonde in a string bikini caught his eye. She was tan and all natural and, wait a second, was that—? It was! In the chair next to her, wearing Ray-Bans and holding a drink with a little umbrella in it was Gorpp!

To that day, Ernie still had no idea how Gorpp traveled, where he stayed, what he ate, or where he came from. He'd also never seen him show any interest in women. Until now. Now, Gorpp had a California girl on both arms. He was a celebrity. Living the high life. It was the damnedest thing Ernie had ever seen. And he had seen some things in close to fifty years in the wrestling business.

Ernie stood there with his hands on the railing. Soaking in the sun in California felt different from Florida somehow. The salt air smelled better. He wasn't generally a contented person. He lived in a state of agitation. He smoked cigarettes and drank instant coffee all day. He always had the jitters. He had hypertension. But standing there looking out at his star attraction soaking up some sun and some affection from the locals gave him a feeling of contentment altogether alien to him.

Then something even stranger happened.

A guy in mechanics' overalls with an odd gait and a cap pulled down over a big head of hair walked right up to Gorpp, leaned over and said something to him. The conversation Ernie couldn't hear at the time went like this:

"Sir, I'm with the, uh, motor club. I understand your vehicle's navigation is malfunctioning."

Gorpp didn't respond. But the look on his face said enough. Even with sunglasses on.

Ernie couldn't hear their conversation but goose pimples pricked his skin as soon as Mr. Overalls arrived. He didn't fit in. Something didn't seem right about him.

"Not me, pal," said Gorpp. He sounded phony.

"You are not Gorpp?" said Overalls.

Everyone at poolside suddenly put their hands over their ears. After a few seconds, they seemed to collectively snap out of it.

"This is Gorpp the Grappler," said one of Gorpp's suntanned pool friends. "He's the World Heavyweight Champion!" She said that last part loud enough for Ernie to hear. Cheers and claps sounded in response from around the pool.

"He's out of this world!" said another of Gorpp's new friends. They seemed very protective of Gorpp, but Overalls was nonplussed by their displays.

Gorpp, of course, recognized Overalls as a patrol the moment he saw him. He just tried to put off acting on the knowledge until he heard him say his name. Not the crude Earth translation. His actual name.

"Well, I guess if you're already here, let's go take a look."

To his friends' disappointment, Gorpp set his drink down, hopped up and strode off at a good clip with Overalls.

Later, Ernie would look back in astonishment that he actually stood there and watched Gorpp walk away. No one on Earth saw him again for almost a year.

CHAPTER 23

As they got back to Gorpp's perfectly functioning vessel (malfunctioning navigation was the only explanation the patrol could think of for why Gorpp would be here), Gorpp pretended to attack him. Overalls unwittingly played his part beautifully, flailing about, making panicked chirps. Gorpp pulled his hat and wig off, revealing an oversized head and big almond eyes. For just a few seconds it looked like a real scrap and you couldn't tell who had the upper hand.

Gorpp knew his vessel's security sensors would record the faux scuffle. After a few seconds, Gorpp relented and casually entered the vessel. Overalls followed him in and again requested answers. Gorpp ignored him, downloaded the footage to take with him, quickly navigated back to the roof of the Ambassador in Tampa and then disabled all controls other than environment in the vessel. Overalls again requested answers. Gorpp didn't respond. He simply stepped back out of the vessel, locking Overalls inside.

Granted, this wasn't a permanent solution. But just a few minutes of Overalls twiddling his thumbs in Gorpp's transport could mean a whole comeback and second run with the title.

The only thing Gorpp couldn't figure out was how Overalls ended up posing as an Earthling there to repair his vehicle. That was deception. That wasn't like their kind.

Until Gorpp.

CHAPTER 24

Gorpp came in the front lobby of the Bayfront Armory right at ten o'clock on a Tuesday morning. In his time, he got Overalls stowed away in his ship in just a few minutes, but to Ernie and other Earthlings, the World Champion simply got up and walked away from a poolside suntanning session with some of the local lovelies, and vanished for more than eleven months. Abandoning the world title he'd been so dogged in pursuing.

Gorpp heard Bobby hollering at some of the boys working out in the ring. He looked up and saw a poster from his first match, against "Mr. America" Mark Carter, right here at the Bayfront, back when Gorpp was still a heel.

He pulled back the curtain and started descending the bleachers. A wrestler he didn't recognize pointed at him from the ring. They all stopped what they were doing and watched Gorpp make his way down the bleachers and walk straight into Mr. Cantrell's office.

Inside the office, Gorpp sat down next to what looked like the same pile of folders and papers and promo photos he'd seen the last time he and Ernie were in this windowless office together. The two looked at each other for some time before either spoke. Ernie, dragging on his cigarette, Gorpp sitting perfectly still but alert.

Gorpp pulled out a device Ernie had never seen before and played him the few seconds of video of him and his doppelganger seemingly slugging it out on the roof of a building. "The angle," Gorpp explained, "is my evil twin brother has come to Earth to seek vengeance on me for allying with your planet. The reason for my disappearance is that he kidnapped me but I've finally broken free and I'm back to reclaim my title."

The evil twin angle.

It was a popular trope from science fiction to soap operas. Gorpp's instinct, that led him to do what he did, told Ernie Gorpp had the potential to be a booker, even run his own territory. He was taking to the business in and out of the ring.

Gorpp later learned that after his unexplained disappearance, they declared the title vacated. They staged another tournament to decide the new Champion. John White Eagle got over ok with the crowd, but the governing body that made up all the territories decided the time had come to give Dimitri a run as a babyface Champion.

He'd gone and visited the kid from the hospital who got his nose bloodied during the Gorpp bout, and it turned out to be great PR for him. But they weren't going to let a Russian hold on to the title belt for long, even if he was from Alaska, so in the rematch they had Dimitri get disqualified (showing his true Russkie colors), losing but not being stripped of his title. This set up a third and final winner-takes-all bout that White Eagle won on a clean finish, to carry on the proud tradition of Native American wrestlers like Wahoo McDaniel and Chief Longbow (though he was actually Nicaraguan).

Ernie had several thoughts simultaneously. The first being that Gorpp's idea was brilliant. Boy, oh boy, was this gonna sell. The next was that Gorpp sure had changed since his disappearance. He had never shown the slightest inclination toward booking or angles before. And his final thought was a twist on top, which is that they'd first have Gorpp come back as a heel and double cross White Eagle to steal his title back. Which he did. Then, once Ernie got the crowd really hating Gorpp, they'd reveal that it had actually been the evil twin all along. That's when they'd use the footage of the scuffle. Later, Gorpp could report he'd escaped and they could make the switch back to babyface. They let him keep the title and Gorpp was so over, the fans never even made a fuss about it.

Everything went according to plan. Gorpp was over as a heel and a babyface. He had the title back. And crowds loved the evil twin storyline. White Eagle wasn't happy, but Ernie was making so much money with Gorpp, he could hardly worry about that. Ernie even got Gorpp to start doing some worked matches, mainly to keep the rest of his stable out of the ER. Gorpp hit all the major territories from Charlotte to Portland, then did his first tour of Japan.

There, the legend of Gorpp had been two years in the making. Crowds in Japan were huge, and they were terrified of Gorpp, heel or babyface. They crossed the street when they saw him coming.

Akana Sato, the Red Dragon, was the biggest wrestler in Japan when Gorpp did his tour. Sato squared off against this invader from another world at the famous Budokan arena in Chiyoda, Tokyo.

No one thought to tell Gorpp about the Red Dragon's gimmick of breathing fire during his ring walk. This time he did it right as he entered the ring (he entered second, even though he was the challenger, since this was his home turf). As soon as the flame erupted from Sato's mouth, Gorpp spit something with incredible force and precision that immediately extinguished the flame. A hush fell over the already polite and quiet crowd.

It immediately became clear, to everyone but Gorpp, that extinguishing the Red Dragon's flame was taken as a deep insult and lack of respect. The language barrier between Ernie and Sato's management with Heavyweight Championship Wrestling from Japan made it a little iffy to begin with, but the match was supposed to be a work with Gorpp getting disqualified. Sato could win in front of his home crowd, but the title would return to the States where fans would never hear about what happened in Japan. Sato came out shooting and paid a price for it when Gorpp put him in the flying saucer and sent him sailing into a crowd of his terrified countrymen who never again saw the Red Dragon as invincible. This took some smoothing over with Sam Calvin, but for the most part, he sided with Gorpp, the money machine.

There was another big change with Gorpp.

He informed Ernie that until further notice he would no longer be making his own travel arrangements. On the stateside and Japanese tours, he drove, flew and stayed with the boys. He hadn't traveled with them since his first matches in the Florida territory.

Even with Gorpp availing himself of more traditional travel stipends, Ernie continued to make good money. When they flew back home from Japan, Gorpp was exhausted, but he realized he didn't have anywhere to go, even back "home" in Tampa, what with Overalls still locked up in his vessel on the roof of the Ambassador. Gorpp exhibited another flash of spontaneity when he took some of his newfound pocket money Ernie had pressed into his palm at the airport, caught a cab and checked in to the upscale Don CeSar on St. Pete Beach. No one asked World Heavyweight Champion Gorpp the Grappler for ID.

Gorpp sat by the pool outside the pink castle of a hotel and watched an Earth wedding. The breeze from the ocean added a certain ambiance to the proceedings. Musicians in matching black tuxedos rounded out the aesthetic. As Gorpp listened to the trill of the bride's laugh move through the salt air like a mirthful current, his mind drifted to the idea of a romantic connection with an Earthling. The next image that entered his mind was of Firefly leaping, as she did at the end of each match, from the top turnbuckle for a crossbody block and pin of her opponent. Her finisher, as they called it in the business. In his mind, Gorpp waited below, and when her body met with his, he caught her in midair and held her close to him.

CHAPTER 25

THE NEXT DAY, Gorpp decided he needed to check on Overalls. While it would only seem like he'd been locked in the transport for a few of his minutes in their time, to Gorpp, who felt more human every day, it felt like he'd left him in there for a year, and he had started to feel antsy about it. That, and he didn't like not having his own transportation and lodging.

Gorpp left his drink on a small serving table by the pool and made his way to the concierge desk. He had gotten used to being stared at and responding with a nod to the frequent greetings from fans. Thankfully, most weren't brave enough to ask for an autograph from the champ.

"I need transportation to the Ambassador Hotel in Tampa," Gorpp said to the nervous concierge.

"Right away, sir," he said. "I'd be honored to drive you myself. I can take you right now." The concierge motioned a bit frantically to one of his coworkers, then walked at a brisk pace out to the circular drive in front of the historic hotel, asked Gorpp to wait "just a moment" then jogged off to retrieve a black Continental to escort the champ in.

When they arrived, the concierge promptly hopped out and ran around to open the door for Gorpp, but when he did, the back seat was empty, apart from an absurd amount of cash left on the seat as a tip.

CHAPTER 26

Gorpp slipped into the alley behind the Ambassador and scaled up the wall to the roof. He moved the old tarps that had covered his vessel, and triggered the doors to unlock and open. He stood outside and a moment later, Overalls emerged, looking just as he had when he trapped him inside back in California.

His temperament hadn't changed. He didn't seem agitated. He simply said to Gorpp, "explain your actions."

So, Gorpp did. From the beginning. He was conscious of not going on too long in Earth time (didn't want to vacate his title again) but he told Overalls of his secret plan to best Earth's Champion and return a conquering hero. He told him about his rise in the ranks of professional wrestling and how he'd been taken under the wing of Ernie Cantrell. He shared with Overalls the epiphany he'd had, when he realized the title didn't represent what he thought it did in terms of their mission here. Then, he shared with him his second epiphany, that he wanted it anyway and that in the Earth-time that had passed since their last encounter, that feeling had only grown stronger. He told Overalls that instead of being a mindless drone and replaceable cog in the machinery of their occupation and invasion force, he had become a respected member of this, albeit primitive, society. He was somebody. He was treated with respect, even with reverence. He told Overalls he may have developed feelings for a female Earthling. He told him everything he could think of to explain why he had disobeyed his orders, changed course and not returned despite the fact his vessel's navigation system was functioning properly. Gorpp's hope was that this deluge of information would be so unusual and challenging to process, report, analyze and respond to that it could mean a lifetime to live on Earth before they sent another patrol.

When Gorpp finished unburdening himself, explaining himself and justifying himself, Overalls didn't respond. He simply stood for a few more moments regarding Gorpp. Once it was clear Gorpp had finished answering the question, Overalls turned and left, presumably to go back to his own vessel and return to Central Command to report this most unusual tale. Gorpp never did learn how Overalls made it from Tampa back to his own vessel in California. It was quite some Earth-time before he heard from Overalls again.

CHAPTER 27

In 1977, Elvis Presley died aged forty-two, *Star Wars* premiered, the Apple II computer went on sale and Ernie's counterparts in other territories were starting to grumble about Gorpp sucking all the life—and revenue—out of the wrasslin' business.

In short, no one could come up with a plausible storyline that fans would believe could actually result in Gorpp losing the title. So, after the novelty wore off, where was the suspense? And a couple of the old timers in particular, egged on by Earl Kruddup, Jr., didn't appreciate the evil twin storyline. They thought it was a slap in the face after Gorpp had already sucked up so much of the money that, instead of using it to get another guy over, they made his arch enemy himself!

When Ernie bought his plane ticket to the annual owners' meeting in St. Louis, he knew he had to show up with a good idea for how Gorpp could drop the belt before the year was out. His willingness to spread the wealth wouldn't be enough. He needed to have a pitch that first, the other owners would buy, and then the fans would buy. Because if they're not buying tickets, nothing else matters.

It ended up being over late night coffee at a Cuban joint in Ybor City that Ernie and Bobby worked out the angle.

CHAPTER 28

ERNIE WAVED Gorpp into his office. The fan blew the hot air and small slips of paper around Ernie's cluttered desk. Gorpp sat and looked at Ernie.

"Listen, son. I need you to drop the title."

Gorpp didn't respond.

"I'm getting too much grief from the other territories. And I don't blame 'em. You're sucking up all the oxygen, all the money. We gotta give 'em some breathing room, so I'm gonna need you to do a job. Me and Bobby got it all figured."

Still no response.

"Do you know what I mean when I say I need you to do a job? It means you need to let the other fella win. Let me walk you through it. We'll start giving White Eagle a push, two, maybe three weeks at home in Miami, then use that to send him out for a few big matches in the Garden, maybe one on the west coast. Then, we'll bring him back here as the former champ and rightful contender for another title shot. We'll have it outside and we'll make damn sure it's been raining. Now, the gimmick is we're gonna have White Eagle do some rain dance and it's gonna get in your head real bad. It'll be something Gorpp the Grappler ain't never seen before, see?

You'll be off balance all night, but it'll be a hard fought contest, seesawing back and forth. Then, he'll do his rain dance, get the crowd into it and get a clean pin on you. We can sell it. Then, we'll have him take the belt on a tour around the other territories. I can work out with the owners who he'll drop it to, but they're not gonna stand for the title staying in Florida forever."

Ernie didn't know how Gorpp would react but he needed him to have some reaction so he knew where they stood.

He didn't.

"Son, I need you to drop the title. At least for a while. You understand?"

No response.

CHAPTER 29

THE RUNUP WENT AS PLANNED. White Eagle had been popular in Miami since the '60s and he still drew money. The road matches ended up being more trouble than they were worth but White Eagle got a good picture in *World Wrestling Digest*. He got to have his son come and see him wrestle at the Garden, and he got that catamaran he'd had his eye on.

Ernie got his wish when it came to the weather the night of the title bout in Miami. The outer bands of a tropical storm wreaking havoc in the Caribbean had the rain flying sideways in Miami.

It was perfect.

White Eagle sold the rain dance storyline and Mother Nature did the rest. Ernie gave Gorpp a stern reminder about the finish for the match, but right up to the ring walks he couldn't elicit a response from him.

John White Eagle handed his headdress to his manager at ringside just as the bell rang to start the match. He'd been wrestling long enough to know the moment he made eye contact with Gorpp that the only way he could win the belt back that night would be if he took it. And White Eagle started shooting.

He was focused and determined, and he'd learned a thing or two from being in the ring with Gorpp before. And, for whatever reason, Gorpp did seem somewhat distracted and off his rhythm. They fought back and forth but in the end, White Eagle just wasn't any match for Gorpp.

Ernie and Bobby grew increasingly uneasy at ringside, as did Steve Levey and the referee. They could all tell this wasn't following the script. Ernie and Bobby considered some kind of improvised screw job or double cross, but they didn't want to burn their bridges with Gorpp, and they didn't want to interrupt a great match the crowd was on the edge of their seats watching.

About forty-five minutes in, Gorpp got White Eagle up and in position for his finishing move—the dreaded flying saucer—but White Eagle's manager threw in the towel. The referee looked to Ernie who waved for him to stop it before White Eagle, or someone in the crowd, got hurt. The ref hesitated but then ran up and clenched Gorpp, stopping the match just before he started spinning.

Gorpp retained his title by forfeit, but White Eagle didn't lose face with his home crowd. They blamed it on his manager. So it was a push. Ernie stopped the screw job Gorpp pulled on him from being a total disaster, but he still hadn't figured out what to do when he got to St. Louis.

CHAPTER 30

Bobby gave a couple knocks on Ernie's office door, then swung it open with his foot and set down two Styrofoam cups of coffee on a pile of papers on his desk. Bobby looked back over his shoulder, all twitchy like.

"There's an investigator here from Tampa PD," Bobby said. "Says he's looking for Gorpp."

Ernie didn't respond. He just got up and walked out of his office, found the plain clothes cop walking around the ring.

"Help you?" Ernie asked, even gruffer than usual.

"I'm looking for one of your—"

"He ain't here."

"You didn't even let me—"

"He ain't here."

"All right. When do you suppose *he* might be back?"

"Couldn't say."

"Do you have an address for him?"

Ernie chuckled. "I do not."

The cop shook his head, sighed, then smiled at Ernie. "All right. Listen, I'm here following up on a lead from the Mobile, Alabama Police Department about a missing person, a wrestler by the name of Robert Graham, went by Buddy. Buddy Graham. You know him?"

"I know of him."

"Mr.?"

"Cantrell."

The cop made a note on his pad. "Mr. Cantrell, do you know what obstruction of justice is?"

"You wanna search my office?" Ernie said. "Go ahead." He motioned to the door. Bobby laughed. Ernie couldn't find anything in his own damn office other than his coffee, his cigarettes and the safe.

"I'll be back," the cop said.

"Buy a ticket next time," Ernie said to his back as he started up the bleachers. That night, he and Bobby were back in Ybor City, drinking Cuban coffee and coming up with a new angle.

CHAPTER 31

The Evil Twin Returns!

First, Gorpp and Firefly disappear.

Then, they get a grainy video of Gorpp's evil twin (really it's Gorpp) saying he's taken Gorpp and Firefly this time (this can start another storyline with a beauty and the beast angle) and he's recruited lieutenants throughout the territories to be his enforcers. This would help draw heat and sell tickets in *all* the territories.

That would play well in St. Louis.

Gorpp could lay low for a while, rest up and just send in the occasional promo. Firefly could work in some other territories under other names for a while.

All Ernie could do then was wait for Gorpp to show up and see if he felt any differently about a hiatus, knowing the cops were looking for him. And he wouldn't have to job a match and lose in a clean finish.

CHAPTER 32

Ernie stood outside barking at Bobby who was up on a ladder changing the sign for that Saturday's card. When he saw Gorpp approach, he left Bobby to it and greeted Gorpp with a nod, took a quick look around, then motioned him into the lobby. They hadn't seen each other since the White Eagle debacle. Ernie stopped and faced Gorpp as soon as the glass door swung shut behind them.

"We got trouble," he said.

Gorpp just looked at him.

"Had a cop sniffing around here looking for you."

Gorpp didn't respond, but Ernie could see his large black eyes dilate.

"Said they want to talk to you about the wrestler copying your shtick up in Alabama. Seems he's turned up missing."

Gorpp turned and pushed his way back through the door and started down the sidewalk in the same direction he'd come. Ernie followed him outside. He and Bobby, still up on the ladder, looked at each other, and by the time they turned back to Gorpp he was gone.

CHAPTER 33

Ernie ambled back inside, held the handrail as he made his way down the bleachers, closed his office door, lit a cigarette and picked up his black rotary phone. He squinted at Howie's number at *World Wrestling Digest* that he had stuck up on the wall with a thumbtack years ago, and dialed.

They talked through the angle Ernie and Bobby came up with for more than an hour. Howie knew a good story when he heard it, and this would be on the cover for sure.

Ernie called Hank Frizzel in the Carolina territories. They worked out a swap where Frizzel would send one of his featured lady wrestlers, Katie Camaro, down to Florida for a run in exchange for Firefly (wrestling under the name "High-flying" Barbi Barnum). Fans didn't care too much who the ladies were; if they looked good in wrestling tights and could move around the ring, they got over. Firefly had no complaints about the change in scenery as long the paychecks kept coming steady. Ernie assured her Frizzel wouldn't short her and he didn't.

A week later Bobby brought the mail in and dropped the new *Digest* on Ernie's desk.

THIS TIME GORPP AND FIREFLY KIDNAPPED BY CHAMP'S EVIL TWIN

Ernie imagined Sam Calvin, Kruddup, Jr., Hank Frizzel and the rest of the owners getting the same issue in the mail. Ernie didn't know if he'd ever see Gorpp again, but he knew his trip to St. Louis would be a hell of a lot less contentious and a lot more interesting now.

CHAPTER 34

Gabby Miller was Firefly's real name.

It was a nine hour drive from Tampa to Charlotte, but Gabby didn't mind. Some of her fondest memories were of the day she just up and left her perfectly planned life in Buckhead in Atlanta where she grew up and started driving. They pushed her to compete at the highest levels of gymnastics from the time she was little. She got really good, but grew more and more resentful of having every aspect, every moment, every movement of her life controlled.

When she turned seventeen, one day on the way home from the gym, she just got on the highway and kept driving. It was after nine at night when she left the gym. She wouldn't have gotten home until close to ten and she would still have homework to do. She was an honors student. But on that night, she just kept driving.

As Gabby passed through Montgomery, her mother started making calls. The gym had closed. Her coach didn't answer. Gabby's mother didn't want to call the police, but she was really starting to worry. By the time her father got in the car and started retracing what would have been her most likely route home from the gym, Gabby was reclining on the warm hood of her BMW, watching the moonlight dance on the surf on Pensacola Beach.

She watched the sunrise still sitting on the hood of her car. Then she went and found a payphone outside of a convenience store and made a collect call to Dr. and Mrs. Miller of Buckhead Manor, to let them know she was alive and she wasn't coming home. Her father made the obligatory noises about coming to drag her back if he had to, but they all knew she turned eighteen in just a couple months, so it just amounted to bluster.

When Gabby's birthday rolled around she was living with a couple roommates, waiting tables at a restaurant called the Silver Slipper in Tallahassee. She was cute and quick on her feet, and if she put up with the occasional pat on the ass from the lobbyists and legislators that hung out there, she made pretty good tips. Her father called on her birthday and informed her he'd set up a bank account she could access if she wanted to continue her education. It would include living expenses on campus, tuition, books, whatever she needed.

Dr. Miller didn't realize Gabby had moved to Tallahassee because of Florida State University's Flying High Circus. Within a couple weeks, Gabby had passed her audition for the Flying High Circus—with "flying colors," her new coach said—and moved into Jennie Murphree Hall at Florida State. It was a small room, but she had it to herself. She spent the days flying through the air without all the pressure from her parents and coaches. One of the male students who had a crush on her dubbed her Firefly. She realized, after a while, she wouldn't be getting her AA and she wouldn't be going to work in the circus, so she decided to turn off the spigot of Daddy's money and get back on the road.

She got on Highway 20 and headed east until it turned into 98 South. She didn't remember how she ended up waiting tables at a bar in West Tampa, not far from Bayfront Armory, but that's where she met Bobby. He'd come in after the matches at the Armory with some of the other wrestlers. She knew there were usually plenty of women waiting for the wrestlers in the parking lot after the matches, but she also knew he was sweet on *her*.

He didn't hit on her and she didn't feel any chemistry with him, but they did end up becoming friends enough that she'd have a drink with him and the boys now and then. One night, they got to talking, and Bobby said they were looking for women wrestlers.

"Gabby here is a gymnast," her boss, the owner of the place, said from behind the bar.

"Bullshit," Bobby said, incredulously. He looked at Gabby. She just shot him a quick smile.

"Oh yeah," her boss continued. "She even went to some circus school up in Tallahassee or something like that."

Bobby brought his new prodigy down to the Armory to audition for Ernie the next day. One look at her leaping from the top turnbuckle and the Firefly was born.

By 1976, she was a regular on Ernie's cards. Lately, she'd gotten some great bookings riding the coattails of Gorpp the Grappler, but it felt good to have the wind back in her hair. She kept the top down from Ocala to Savannah, stopped for lunch at a little sidewalk café downtown and then pushed on to Charlotte.

CHAPTER 35

Life on the road in the territories was hard living. Taking hard bumps. Doctoring your own wounds when the lights went down and the crowd was only an echo in your head. Sometimes, you were lucky to break even after buying gas and fixing flats and eating fast food in the car on your way to the next card. And sometimes you got stiffed altogether by a sleazy promoter and you ended up paying for the privilege to wrestle. That's how it went for the guys.

The women had it harder.

Gabby and her opponent were often the only women on the card. The guys were already sharing a small locker room and shower—one for the babyfaces, one for the heels. That meant no locker room at all for the women. Gabby had stopped even complaining about having to sneak into a stall in the women's facilities the crowd used, and trying to get into her tights with puddles of piss and pools of vomit on the floor around her. Most of the promoters, most of the wrestlers, and most of the crowd were men, and they were all working each other up into a frenzy when they got together in the armories, high school gyms and sometimes, like in Tallahassee, the warehouses they wrestled in. And, as often as not, the lot of them were drunk. If Gabby hadn't been tough she wouldn't have survived. But she'd taken her share of hard bumps in and out of the ring.

In Charlotte, Hank Frizzel had built up a good stable of talent, he managed his business well and had a loyal fan base. He kept his word to Ernie to give Gabby a fair shake. She'd wrestled in Charlotte and worked in the surrounding territories, with different opponents in spot shows in what Frizzel thought of as satellites.

After the card in Charlotte, she took a hot shower in the arena locker room, toweled off, dressed and grabbed her duffel, then headed to her car. She was one of the last to leave. Gabby waved goodnight to a janitor and heard a couple people yelling back and forth about who would be cleaning the latrines. She pushed through the back door of the arena and found herself confronted by a much darker parking lot than she remembered coming into. She paused in the doorway, looked up at the lamppost and saw the light had burned out.

Not great timing.

Gabby marched resolutely out toward her car as if she were braving a snowstorm. Even professional wrestlers don't like to walk to their cars alone at night when they're women. When she got within a few feet of her Mustang, she saw his shape take form out of the darkness.

Gorpp.

"Oh my God!" Gabby pushed her palms into his chest hard enough to knock her typical opponent flat on their ass, but Gorpp only slightly budged. She'd never had reason to touch him before but she was immediately taken aback by his uncanny strength and balance. She looked down and tried to relax her clenched shoulders. She picked up her duffel she didn't remember having dropped. "You scared the shit out of me," she said. "What are you doing here?"

"I came to see you."

CHAPTER 36

Gabby wasn't in the habit of getting in a car with a guy she didn't really know, but on impulse, she asked him to go back with her to the apartment she was staying in. Gorpp didn't verbally respond. He just walked around to the passenger side of the car and climbed in. Gabby got in the driver's seat and soon they were on their way with the top down.

She put the radio on a classic rock station and felt a little like a North Carolina Jackie-O who liked to sing along with Tom Petty and the Heartbreakers. Gabby looked down to turn up the volume on "American Girl" and noticed something that should have been the most normal thing in the world—this world anyway—but struck her as just about the strangest thing she'd ever seen. Gorpp was tapping his foot in time with the beat.

Back at Gabby's apartment, Gorpp declined her offer of a beer. Gabby put the radio back on and sat down next to him on the couch. She slapped his knee.

"I knew there was something different about you. I've never seen you in street clothes," she said. Gorpp was wearing Nikes, Levi's, a black t-shirt and a windbreaker.

He didn't respond.

"Do you want to hear some gossip?" she asked, and he turned to face her. "Dimitri is leaving the Florida territory. He and that manager of his weren't too happy about the match he had with you, and then having to job his title away to Johnny, you know?"

Gorpp didn't respond.

"Anyway, Dimitri and Alexi made a deal with Kruddup's asshole son to do a babyface run with the Southeast title in his territory. I bet Ernie's got steam coming out of his ears." She could tell Gorpp had no interest. Gabby took a sip of her beer and put it down on the coffee table. "So, you came all the way to Charlotte to see me?"

"Yes."

CHAPTER 37

EARL KRUDDUP, Jr. ran the Southeast territory from a doublewide trailer in an industrial park on the outskirts of Mobile. Alexi turned off the highway into the unpaved driveway leading up to the unmarked headquarters of their new employer. Alexi looked at Dimtri as doubts started to run through both of their minds about the tradeoff they'd made.

They parked in a cloud of dust, got out and put their boots down into sand. Then, the trailer door opened and there stood Junior.

"Gentlemen, welcome to Alabama! Welcome to Heavyweight Championship Wrestling of the Southeast! Come on in." Kruddup had suspenders, a bow tie and a fancy cane. He was a young man, but he had a limp, a lazy eye and a combover. The Russians couldn't stand him right from the start.

Outside, it was hot and humid. Inside Kruddup's trailer it was hot and stuffy and smelled faintly of garbage that had been sitting. Kruddup had an oscillating fan blowing little scraps of paper around on his desk just like Ernie did. Dimitri and Alexi sat in metal folding chairs across from Kruddup's desk.

"Alright, gentlemen. We've got a few papers to sign, then we're off to the races. Dimitri, I'm cooking up a big welcome to Southeast for you. I'm thinking of putting you in a cage match with the Masked Bandit. We'll call it 'The Battle of the Berlin Wall.' By the end of the year, we'll have you over, and you can take the belt off of Billy Bronco. Then, we'll send you all over the territory to defend it. Lake Charles, Lafayette, Baton Rouge, Biloxi, Hattiesburg, then over to Pensacola, Panama City and Tallahassee."

The Russians looked at each other again.

"Isn't that Ernie's territory?" Alexi asked.

"I won't tell if you won't," Kruddup said. Then he turned and yelled into a back room. "Carol, get us some coffee in here, would you?"

CHAPTER 38

THEY DIDN'T EXACTLY ROLL out the welcome mat for Ernie in St. Louis. A few of the other owners looked up and one gave a nod when he entered the conference room. Ernie stepped to the back, got a cup of coffee and then proceeded to the tables that had been arranged in a squared circle, fitting for this gathering.

Their president, Sam Calvin, gaveled them to order with a few clinks of his spoon on the edge of a carafe of water. "Good morning. This, the thirtieth annual meeting of the owners of Heavyweight Championship Wrestling, is now convened. Our first order of business is the vacant world title. There have been a number of scenarios brought to my attention prior to this meeting—"

"Let's just make sure our next champ is from Earth," came a voice from the far side of the table. Ernie looked up from his coffee, but didn't see who said it. He just heard the murmur of chuckles and felt a few glares in his direction.

Nat Pfeifer from the Minnesota territory wanted his top guy, Bear Claw Monroe to get the nod. Someone suggested giving old Black Jack Tolliver a chance at redemption, but this wasn't a sentimental crowd. By lunchtime, a blue-gray cloud of cigarette and cigar smoke hovered like a fog over the owners.

Freddy Gallagher had been a top guy in his day in the '40s and '50s at the Olympic Auditorium in Los Angeles. Now, he ran the California territory from San Diego to Santa Barbara. "Look, fellas, I'm no more a fan of little green men than the rest of you, and I certainly think Ernie has sucked up his fair share of our revenues for the past two years, but I have to raise a practical question at this point." He held up a copy of last month's *Digest*. Every owner had, of course, seen it, but they all read the headline again as he held it up.

THIS TIME GORPP AND FIREFLY KIDNAPPED BY CHAMP'S EVIL TWIN

"Howie tells me this is the biggest selling issue he's ever put out. If you fellas had actually read the article, you'd have seen not only that fans are still hooked on this angle, but also that there's now a wrinkle that gives all of us an opening to belly up to the trough. Now, I don't know if this was Ernie's idea or Howie's, and I don't care, but if we keep this thing going we can run an angle where our top heels are in league with this evil twin, and maybe we start putting some asses in the stands again." Gallagher tossed the magazine aside and the room fell quiet as men sipped their lukewarm coffee and lit another round of cigarettes, cigars and a pipe or two.

Sam Calvin tried to get all the owners rowing in the same direction, but as always, some went along and some didn't. Two days later, when Ernie got back in a cab headed for St. Louis International, some of the owners were on board to play out the evil twin thread and see if they could use it to get some heat on their top heels. Others decided to pretend the story in last month's *Digest* never happened and see if fans pushed back. Calvin ended up going along with some gimmick to put the belt on Bear Claw Monroe up in Minnesota. What a joke. Every owner knew if Gorpp ever did come back he'd put an end to that charade.

CHAPTER 39

WHEN BUDDY GRAHAM cracked open his crusted eyelids, he found himself hungover, on the floor of a Biloxi hotel room. He'd been on a two week bender.

Buddy hadn't thought much about wrestling, or the night he up and vanished in Mobile. He had no idea there was a missing persons investigation underway. He hadn't given any thought to how upset Sue would be over his disappearance. Though it never occurred to him she would actually think he'd been abducted or even killed by an alien who also happened to be the hottest ticket in professional wrestling. It wouldn't be until later on that those pieces fell into place.

He pulled up into a sitting position and disentangled himself from a sheet he must have pulled down off the bed when he rolled onto the floor. The sheet had an unpleasant stain and odor about it. His back ached, probably from the combination of an old injury, countless body slams and sleeping off a drunk on the hard floor. It would only take an hour to get back to Mobile. If he could remember where he parked. He couldn't wait to see Junior's face when he showed up. There would be no more parading around as a spaceman for that little prick.

CHAPTER 40

WHEN THE PHONE rang it startled Gabby, but Gorpp didn't flinch. "Who in the hell is calling me here at two o'clock in the morning?" She got up and answered the phone, wondering if an obsessed fan had figured out she'd been staying at another wrestler's apartment while he toured in Japan. Right before she picked up, she had a flash of panic that her parents were calling because someone had died.

"Hello?"

"Gabby, this is Rex Miles over at USCW in Louisville. I reached Hank after he got home tonight and he gave me your number."

"USCW?"

"Yeah, Upland South Championship Wrestling. Biggest promotion in the Ohio valley."

"Well, Rex, it's two o'clock in the morning here in Charlotte. What can I do for you?"

"Sorry for the late hour. I hoped I'd catch you still up. I had one of my girls get hurt and I need a fill-in. Hank said I could borrow you for a few shows over here in the Upland South territory. First one is a matinee tomorrow."

Gabby gave Gorpp a *sorry* look and then turned her attention back to the call. "Isn't it like an eight hour drive to Louisville?"

"I bet you can do it in seven. And you'll gain an hour when you cross over to Central Time."

"I'd practically have to get in my car right now and pull an all-night drive."

"That's why I'm calling you at two in the morning. Listen, sweetie, you splash some water on your face, make a pot of coffee and get on the road. I'll make sure Hank knows how much I appreciate it."

Gabby heard the underhanded threat in the subtext, and when she hung up the phone she knew she didn't have much choice but to get back on the road. The conversation about why Gorpp had come to see her would have to wait. She gave a fleeting thought to inviting him to come with her, but quickly dismissed it. Instead, she let him stay at the apartment.

Gabby did pretty much as her new boss instructed. She washed her face, brushed her hair and teeth, got some cash from the ballerina music box on the dresser (she took it with her everywhere), made that pot of coffee, poured it in her thermos and grabbed her duffel. She gave Gorpp a kiss on the cheek and headed out the door. Gabby put the top down on her Mustang, dialed up some Bob Seger on the radio and got on 75-North.

She would enjoy the ride.

CHAPTER 41

SHE SAW the sun rise as she passed through Knoxville. Gabby pulled into the parking lot of Breckinridge High School in Louisville just before eleven. She'd be wrestling in their gymnasium on the noon card. She walked into a sparse crowd and started looking around for someone who could tell her where to change.

"Hey, Rex. Looks like your jabroni girl's here." Gabby turned to see a weaselly looking character adjusting the ring ropes. "You need to put some makeup on, girl. You look like you been up all night."

CHAPTER 42

Gorpp used his time alone in the apartment to plot a comeback. Like any Champion, he wanted to reclaim his title. Gorpp had become something of a student of wrestling. He'd read up on the history. He knew his story would become part of wrestling canon. He felt pride at being a two-time World Heavyweight Champion, even if being Champion of the wrestling world and Champion of Earth weren't the same thing.

That's where he got the idea for his greatest angle.

He decided, instead of going back to Ernie to handle the business end of things, he would become a free agent and cut a promo he would then send directly to the press. He'd decided to use what he'd learned in the world of professional wrestling—where precious little is what it appears to be, except the pain—to save the Earth from invasion.

CHAPTER 43

Earl Kruddup, Jr. got Nat Pfeifer on the phone from the Minnesota territory, though he didn't want to take the call.

"What do you want, Junior?"

"You know what I want, Nat. Come on. We have mutual interests. Southeast is on fire. I'm sure you've heard Dimitri defected from Cantrell's camp and came over to me. I want to do a program with Dimitri and Monroe. Let's make some money together—" Kruddup paused, then instead of going with "Nat," he finished with, "Mr. Pfeifer."

"Mr. Pfeifer? Are you fucking kidding me? Look, kid. Call Calvin. He's the one who schedules the Champion."

"You're full of shit, Nat. You and I both know, at the end of the day, you're calling the shots to protect Bear Claw while Calvin's off in a tanning booth in Tahoe or wherever the hell."

Pfeifer didn't immediately respond, so Kruddup took a different tack. "Listen, I just want to make some money and bring Bear Claw down so our deep south fans can 'hear the bear roar!' And I wouldn't waste your fucking time or mine if I didn't know you and Monroe would make some real money down here. Now goddammit, I'm shooting you straight on this."

"You're a snake, Junior. You're encroaching on Ernie's territory over there in Florida. You're stealing his top guys. I don't trust you. I don't like you. And I don't want anything to do with you." He hung up the phone.

Kruddup took Pfeifer's advice and called Sam Calvin at headquarters in St. Louis. Calvin wasn't the easiest man to get on the phone either, but once Kruddup had him in his clutches, he found Calvin a much easier mark. Junior made a little side deal with Calvin and by the time Pfeifer got wind of the champ's schedule, and the pass he would take through Southeast, the posters were already being printed and the article had already been fed to Howie Shows. Bear Claw would lose face if he pulled out, and Pfeifer felt like Kruddup had wrapped him up in an inside cradle, just like Gorpp did when he took the title from Dimitri. Being played like that by a little punk like Earl Kruddup, Jr. left Pfeifer feeling old and slow. He had a bad feeling about this trip down to the deep south.

CHAPTER 44

Between Calvin and Pfeifer, they had Bear Claw on the road constantly. But nobody's box office could compete with Gorpp's and his two runs with the belt. There were letters from fans in the *Digest* saying the only reason people bought tickets to a Bear Claw match was because they thought they might get to see the title change hands.

And this month, Howie would run a story to help plant the seed for the Southeast angle where Dimitri was the babyface visiting children's hospitals and Bear Claw turns heel, at least for the Southeast run, to build up Dimitri.

Now, of course no one, not Sam Calvin, not Nat Pfeifer, and certainly not Bear Claw Monroe would have agreed to any angle where he dropped the belt to Dimitri Drozdov, especially not with Dimitri working for Earl Kruddup, Jr. But Dimitri was a hooker in his prime and Bear Claw would be no match for him in a shoot.

CHAPTER 45

DIMITRI PACED BACK and forth waiting for Bear Claw Monroe to make his ring walk. He came out high-stepping, looking pretty spry for a guy who'd been taking bumps for going on thirty years now. He did his trademark move of stepping over the top rope to get into the ring, then letting out a loud roar. Dimitri kept pacing.

They'd met earlier in a small room with a **JANITOR'S SUPPLIES** sign on the door—the designated kayfabe consult room at the newly named Mobile Sportatorium. The name did little to make up for the fact it was just an old warehouse with folding chairs, no AC and bad lighting. Bear Claw gave Dimitri the run of show, walked him through a few spots, and he promised he'd sell for him so, even in losing, Dimitri would get over with his newly adopted hometown crowd. Dimitri nodded, saying little. He avoided eye contact with the Champion.

Once the bell rang, they circled, clenched and, as they'd discussed, Bear Claw used his considerable height and weight advantage to push Dimitri across the ring onto his ass after the break the first few times they locked up. Bear Claw followed that up with a series of headlocks on the challenger that he capped off with a big pounding fist to the top of the head that dropped Dimitri to his knees. The Champion grabbed him by the hair and hoisted him up, then did it again.

On the third attempt, Dimitri grabbed hold of Bear Claw's knees. He teetered, then, like a big tree, fell with a crash to the canvas. This got a rise out of the crowd and seemed to spur Dimitri to a comeback. He jumped on the Champion, applied his own headlock and started grinding on Bear Claw's big shaggy head. The champ sold for him, waving his arms frantically to show his pain and distress with the tables turned. That's when Dimitri went off script.

He quickly released Bear Claw from the headlock, shimmied behind him and applied an armbar—one of the most basic and most painful holds in wrestling. Monroe had a bad right shoulder. Everybody knew it. Dimitri applied pressure, driving that bad shoulder into Bear Claw's ear. The Champion went from selling to crying out in real pain. Sweat broke out on his forehead and he twisted his mouth close to Dimitri's ear.

"Let up! That's my bad shoulder. Let up!"

Dimitri turned his face away and doubled down. Bear Claw's cries of anguish were difficult to listen to, but Dimitri couldn't back out now. When Monroe started whimpering, Dimitri turned back to him.

"I'm taking the belt," he whispered through clenched teeth. "Do you want to submit or do you want me to pin you?"

His face ground into the mat, Bear Claw didn't answer. Dimitri redoubled his efforts and they both heard something tear in Bear Claw's shoulder. Mickey, the referee, who was in on the double cross (and would be getting a new Jet Ski soon, courtesy of Junior) waved it off, telling the officials at ringside Bear Claw had conceded. The bell rang with Bear Claw Monroe in no position to dispute the call. He lay in a pile on the mat as the ref handed the world title to Dimitri and raised his hand in victory.

Nat wasn't even surprised when he got the call from Monroe later that night from Providence Hospital in Mobile. "They fucked me, Nat. Kruddup's kid, the Russians. The ref. They were all in on it. You were right. I should've listened to you…" Monroe's words drifted off and Pfeifer realized his old friend, Robert Monroe from up in Saskatchewan, whose career he'd helped guide and promote for all these years until they finally got to the top, had just ended in Mobile, Alabama.

"Robert, did they hurt you?"

He just heard sobs in the phone coming from Providence Hospital. He'd tried to stop it but he'd failed. He'd failed his friend, and the double cross at Southeast would mark the beginning of the end of both Pfeifer and Monroe's careers in professional wrestling.

CHAPTER 46

Junior leaned back in his leather executive office chair and leered at Carol's backside as she bent over to get something out of the metal file cabinet. He imagined the way her body would move on his waterbed.

He had the title back at Southeast for the first time since his father, the Earl Kruddup at least some men in wrestling respected, had a Champion from Southeast. That had been back in 1953. And it hadn't lasted long.

The way Junior saw it, the owners from the other territories—from the East Coast big city boys to the West Coast suntan pretty boys—had always looked down on his family. They looked down on their heritage, their accents and their intelligence. And especially him. Junior didn't believe they'd really respected his father all that much, either. They threw him a bone so he'd play ball. But he had never been in their club. His dad never talked about it, but Junior knew. Well, Junior wasn't going to eat their shit and smile anymore. He'd keep taking more of Ernie's Florida territory and talent until he had the entire Southeast—from New Orleans to Key West. And that would just be another crown in the jewel of the empire he'd build around his new World Champion. Junior figured his well laid plans were paying dividends, just as he knew they would. He didn't give a shit if the way he did it pissed off old Nat Pfeifer or any of the other dinosaurs running this monopoly, this crime family called Heavyweight Championship Wrestling. He didn't remember signing up to play by their rules and he'd be damned if he would do it anymore. No honor among thieves, as they say. Pretty soon he'd be the one running the whole show, and if Sam Calvin wanted a suntan he'd have to go sit the fuck outside like the rest of them.

"Hey, sugar," he said to Carol, "I dropped my pen. Why don't you bend over and get it for me?"

CHAPTER 47

NAT PFEIFER DEMANDED Sam Calvin hold a proxy vote of the owners on his motion to have Earl Kruddup Jr. barred, and Southeast to no longer be sanctioned under the auspices of Heavyweight Championship Wrestling until it had new ownership independent of Kruddup. Easier said than done without breaking kayfabe. To the wrestling world, Dimitri taking Bear Claw's title looked like an above board and entirely plausible outcome. They even read about it in *World Wrestling Digest*. Apparently, Junior wasn't quite the fool they made him out to be.

CHAPTER 48

Sam Calvin dreaded making this phone call. But it couldn't all be country clubs and golf courses being the president of Heavyweight Championship Wrestling, whatever the fellas may think. On the fourth ring, he thought maybe he'd get lucky and Pfeifer wouldn't answer, but on the fifth he picked up.

"Thousand Lakes Wrestling," he said.

"Nat. It's Sam."

"What are you doing calling me at six o'clock in the evening?"

"What, did I interrupt goddamn dinner with the wife and kids?"

"I'm watching the evening news. Did you call to tell me you took the vote?"

"Nat, I can't do it. I can't. He's got us by the shorthairs."

Pfeifer didn't respond, but Calvin heard the monotone of the evening news anchor in the background.

"I'm sorry, Nat."

Calvin heard the voice on Pfeifer's television change to a younger, more energetic correspondent. He caught something about standing in front of the White House.

"Sam, turn on your television."

"What?"

"Turn on your goddamn television, the evening news with Marvin Castle. Turn it on now!" Pfeifer sounded like he might hyperventilate.

Calvin put the phone down, got up and walked around his desk to turn on the big Zenith he had on his credenza. He put it on channel four. When the picture tubes warmed up and he had a clear image, he saw a young reporter with a microphone standing in front of the White House.

"Ever since Roswell, Americans have asked, if there really are UFOs and aliens here from other worlds, why wouldn't they land on the White House lawn and make their presence known? Well, I have with me here tonight, live from in front of the White House, former World Champion, Gorpp. And, well, Mr., um, Gorpp has a message for our viewers."

The camera panned out to show Gorpp standing beside the reporter. He wore jeans, a black leather jacket and a scarf. "People of Earth, I am Gorpp. I am from the ice-covered moon of Enceladus that orbits Saturn. I am here to conquer your world. Dimitri Drozdov," Gorpp pointed a finger at the camera as sternly as he could. "I am coming for you."

"Um, well, that's the news from here. I'm David Rosenblum, reporting live from the White House. Back to you at the studio." Some say Gorpp just seemed to disappear from the shot and that by the time Rosenblum signed off, they saw a small circular disc flash across the sky behind him, right over the White House. The station called it condensation on the cameraman's lens that caught a glint of light. The White House wouldn't comment.

When the shot cut back to the studio, Marvin Castle looked a little unsteady, which was news in and of itself. But he quickly regained his composure. "Well, the aliens have landed on the White House lawn and, wait, is that Bigfoot I see on the grassy knoll in front of the Texas School Book

Depository?" Calvin heard a few uneasy chuckles from off camera.

"I think that about does it for us here tonight," Castle said. "Goodnight and God bless us all." It wasn't his usual sign-off and it left people who saw it feeling a little uneasy.

Most who weren't wrestling fans didn't know the name Dimitri Drozdov, though many people had at least heard of Gorpp. He had dominated headlines in all the tabloids for months, but that had been two years ago. People had mostly written him off as a freak from here on Earth and then forgotten about him. But, inside the wrestling world, where Gorpp's message was really intended, his reappearance and his challenge to the new World Champion—whom he'd defeated before—sent shockwaves.

CHAPTER 49

IT CAME WITH SOME DISAPPOINTMENT, if no surprise, to find Gorpp gone when Gabby returned. He'd left a note for her on the kitchen counter. It simply read, "Mobile."

She'd seen the eleven o'clock version of the story on the news the night before from a cheap motel in Evansville, Indiana.

The ice-covered moon of Enceladus?

This weird business was getting weirder all the time. The weird business of wrestling, of Gorpp, and of life. Gabby put her ballerina box and a few toiletries in her duffel and left Charlotte. It would take eight hours to get to Mobile.

Good thing she liked driving.

CHAPTER 50

DIMITRI AND ALEXI were sharing a doublewide in the Palm Shores Trailer Court. The life of a Champion. Even with the Championship belt locked up in a safe behind a panel of plywood in the kitchen, it still felt like they'd taken a step down from working with Ernie in Florida. The night after Gorpp made the front page of every newspaper in Alabama saying he was coming for Dimitri, they finished a spot show in nearby Biloxi, hit a bar called the Riverboat, then got on the road for home.

It must have been three in the morning when they pulled through the palm tree archway into the trailer court. There were no lights on when they stumbled to the front door, drunk and exhausted. Alexi unlocked the door and they both rumbled inside, only to find Gorpp sitting quietly on their couch.

"We need to talk," Gorpp said.

The Russians held their ground with the still open front door close by, and remained standing. Gorpp started talking.

"We both know you have to give me a shot at the title and that I can take the belt in a straight shoot but that one or both of us is likely to get hurt in the process. Nobody wants that. I have my own reasons for needing the belt back, but I have no, how would you say, quarrel with you. I propose a worked match that ends up with me taking the belt unfairly so we accomplish three things: I get the belt, you save face, and nobody gets hurt."

"What if we say no?" Alexi asked.

"Then I take the belt and somebody probably gets hurt," Gorpp said.

CHAPTER 51

The match could have made more money at Caesars Palace or Madison Square Garden, or at the Olimpiyskiy in Moscow. But, since Kruddup could make more money in his own backyard, the rematch between Drozdov and Gorpp took place right there in Mobile, Alabama. That ought to put a little shine on the new Sportatorium, Junior thought.

He put up a banner on Broad Street:

**1st HEAVYWEIGHT CHAMPIONSHIP IN MOBILE
IN A QUARTER CENTURY
GORPP VS. DROZDOV
SATURDAY, 8 P.M.
AT THE NEW MOBILE SPORTATORIUM!**

Junior jacked up the ticket prices and it still sold out. They had folks coming from as far east as Miami and as far west as Dallas. And, if you believed the evening news, from as far away as the moons of Saturn! That was a good one. He'd make sure and give that as a quote to Howie Shows after the match. If you asked Junior, every restaurant and hotel owner in Mobile should be sending him a thank you card.

He put up another big banner across the front entryway of the Sportatorium that said, **HALL OF CHAMPIONS**. And he raised the prices on hotdogs, popcorn and beer too.

Kruddup's only queasiness stemmed from Gorpp refusing to talk to him directly about the match. Alexi assured him Gorpp and Dimitri had worked out their spots, they were both clear on the finish and he had nothing to worry about.

Well, that's what Bear Claw Monroe thought too.

Gorpp came out to "Flying Saucers Rock-n-Roll" and the packed house shook with the roar of the crowd. Dimitri came out to boos and the national anthem of the Union of Soviet Socialist Republics. Fans in the Bible Belt weren't going for the Russian babyface anyway, and when the rumors started about him purposefully ending Bear Claw's career, Kruddup just decided to lean into it and have Dimitri go full on heel. It would be more fun to have a heel Champion anyway.

Boos filled the Sportatorium and Dimitri got pelted in the side of the head with one of those overpriced hotdogs on his way to the ring. Mustard dripped down his temple but it didn't break his concentration. Then a metal chair sailed by, grazing Alexi's head and opening up a cut that started to drip blood down into his collar. The Russians kept marching to the ring. Almost as an afterthought, before Gorpp had left their trailer, he'd mentioned he would be willing to hand over his paycheck for the match as part of the arrangement. That had sealed the deal for the Russians.

Once both combatants were in the ring, Junior climbed through the ropes and took hold of the microphone dangling from the rafters. He did his own announcing in Southeast. Helped save money and stroked his ego at the same time.

For the first time, Gorpp wore an elaborate white robe to the ring. It was silk with fur lining, rhinestones outlining the lapel and the claim **TRUE CHAMPION** emblazoned across the back.

"Introducing first, in this corner, the former two-time

Heavyweight Champion of the World, and number one contender, from the moons of Saturn, Gooooooorppp!" Thunderous applause greeted Gorpp. And for the first time, he waved to his fans, even took a small bow. They ate it up.

When Gorpp bowed, he saw her standing by the steps in his corner: Gabby, in her full attire as Firefly. He looked at her intently and the crowd noise drifted away, overshadowed by the vision of her standing there.

"I came to see you," she mouthed, pointing first to herself and then to him. Gorpp smiled. It may have been the first time.

"And in this corner, the undisputed *current* Champion of the World, from Moscow in the Soviet Union, Dimitri, 'the Russian Bear' Drooooozzzzzdov!"

Dimitri winced at the underhanded dig at Bear Claw. Not to mention, he was known as the Russian *Blackbird*. He'd never been called the Russian *Bear*. The crowd made their displeasure with their new Champion known. They could more easily imagine Drozdov getting on a 747 back to Mother Russia after the match than riding out to a doublewide in the Palm Shores Trailer Court.

"Tonight's rematch for the world title is one fall with a sixty-minute time limit, and for the first time in a quarter century, it's happening right here in Alabama!"

Just as he finished, Carol showed up frantic at ringside, hollering and waving at Junior. Looked like she was about to blow a gasket. "We can't find Mickey!" she kept saying. "We can't find Mickey!"

Junior hastily scanned the ring. The third man, as the referee is known, was nowhere to be found. Junior climbed out of the ring and started toward Carol.

"He was in back, getting dressed, but now we can't find him," she fretted.

"Here we are, Daddy," Junior said, glancing toward the rafters and crossing his heart. "I got us back to the bigtime and I'm surrounded by the gang that can't shoot straight." He stormed off toward the dressing rooms.

"Mickey! Where's that goddamn referee?"

An unassuming janitor named Wiley Coates, who had a crisp hundred dollar bill in his front right pocket, answered the frantic Kruddup.

"The referee's in that room down there says 'janitor's storage' on the door."

Kruddup shot him an incredulous, almost maniacal look, then stomped down the hall, hollering all the way. He flung the janitor's closet open and burst inside. As soon as he did, Wiley Coates quietly closed the door behind him and locked it. Junior made an awful racket in there, sounded like he was climbing the walls, but Wiley ignored it, made his way back to the entrance to the arena and gave Carol a thumbs up.

That's when Mickey, the same ref from the Bear Claw double cross, slipped into the ring from the other side. This time wearing a patch over his left eye. He brought Champion and challenger together to go over the instructions and check them for foreign objects. Gabby didn't like Gorpp going to the center of the ring alone when Dimitri had Alexi by his side, always whispering, scheming. Firefly hopped into the ring and fell in behind Gorpp as he faced off with Dimitri. The crowd ate it up.

To set up the angle, Alexi kept trying to get the ref's attention to point out something he didn't like about Gorpp's boots, but the ref couldn't see him from the side with the eye patch. Alexi even started waving his hands in the air, but the ref still couldn't see him. Alexi sold it to the crowd and got a few laughs. But, people saw the ref had a blind spot. That was the important thing.

As soon as the bell rang, Dimitri and Gorpp found a good rhythm together. They hit their spots and sold for each other. At one point, Dimitri had Gorpp in a half nelson. He thought about how he'd nearly beaten him that first time at the Omni in Atlanta by repeatedly attacking his rotator cuff, and how he'd ultimately won the title by destroying Bear Claw Monroe's shoulder permanently. But they'd made a deal, and Dimitri intended to honor it. His gut told him Gorpp would too.

At about the twenty-minute mark, Dimitri appeared to be tiring, and Gorpp managed to get him into the flying saucer. Only a few people in the Sportatorium that night had ever seen Gorpp do the flying saucer in person, so most didn't realize it was a slow motion version of it. When he hurled Dimitri over the ropes he fell just outside the ring. When Dimitri climbed back up on the ring apron he was selling the deadlights but Gorpp had seen the real thing before and could tell this was just Dimitri following the script. But Gorpp started backing up, selling his fabricated fear of the Champion.

When Dimitri got a hold of Gorpp, he started pounding him with fists and elbows, punctuated by the well-timed stomping of his boots on the canvass to heighten the effect. Finally, Dimitri flung Gorpp into the ropes, and on his return coldcocked him with a flying drop kick. Gorpp dropped flat on his back and Dimitri scrambled over for the pin, but the ref got distracted by a fight breaking out in the crowd—couple of guys from the undercard staged it in the twelfth row—and he didn't see the pin because of his eye patch.

Alexi was going ballistic in the corner, but the more he yelled the more the ref looked at him and not at the still prone Gorpp who had been pinned for a three count at least three times over.

Right about then, Earl Kruddup, Jr. burst through the janitor's closet door and began racing for the ring in his awkward gait yelling, "Double cross! It's a screw job!" But nobody paid him much mind.

Finally, Dimitri got up, walked over, grabbed the referee's shoulder and spun him around, just in time to see Gorpp leap up, catch Dimitri with his own flying dropkick and then roll him up for the pin. "One—two—three!" The bell rang, and the one-eyed ref raised Gorpp's hand in victory.

Alexi leapt in the ring and did his part, screaming at the seemingly bewildered ref while Dimitri lay still on the canvass. Earl Kruddup, Jr. wasn't an athletic man, far from it, but his rage propelled him into the ring. He'd be damned if he'd take this double cross lying down. The referee raised Gorpp's hand in victory and handed him back his world title belt. The crowd cheered as Gorpp raised the belt over his head, victorious. Kruddup came up behind Gorpp, but just as he reached out for the belt, Firefly came leaping off the top turnbuckle, flew over Gorpp's head and hit Kruddup with a perfectly timed cross body block, sending him crashing to the canvass. When she landed she could feel the breath push out of his diaphragm and a couple of his ribs crack too. Gorpp reached down and helped her up. They made the walk back to the dressing rooms waving to the adoring crowd.

Junior lay on the mat with his broken ribs and the belt headed for God knew where. To have his own guy double cross him by *losing* the title and for Gorpp to play the classic heel role—winning illegitimately—but still win over the crowd? That was a new one on Junior. And Mickey with that fucking eyepatch. Junior had so much anger boiling up in him, for Mickey—with his Jet Ski—and those ungrateful Russians. Even the janitor was on the take.

Jesus, Daddy, Junior thought. They were all against me and I never even saw it coming. He didn't make the connection then that Carol had been in on it too.

But he would.

CHAPTER 52

By the time Junior could hoist himself up into a sitting position, everybody had gone. Gorpp and Firefly, Dimitri and Alexi, Mickey, and even Carol, were gone. He had to get a zit-faced usher to come into the ring and help him to his feet. One of his ribs felt like it might poke out of his side. The usher held his elbow and slowly guided him through the ropes and down the steps onto the floor. As soon as they got there, a rotund fella in a cheap suit chewing on a toothpick ambled up to Kruddup.

"Mr. Kruddup, a word?"

"You Mobile PD? Good. I've got a whole slew of charges to file, starting with assault, against that flying bitch that broke my ribs. And then—"

"Mr. Kruddup, I'm here about our missing persons investigation I spoke with you about—"

"What the hell's that got to do with me?" Kruddup bellowed.

"Sir, I just need to speak with Mr.—" the cop switched the toothpick to the other side of his jowls and looked at his notepad, as if he couldn't remember the name. "—Mr. Gorpp."

Kruddup's trembling mouth twisted into a kind of perverse smile. Maybe there would be some justice here after all. He shifted his tone to one of the accommodating host, even though each inhale caused the jagged edge of a broken rib to poke into his insides.

"Let me take you back to the dressing rooms," Junior said between clenched teeth. "Usher!" he yelled to the boy who'd started sweeping popcorn and cigarette butts from beneath the chairs. "Come give me a hand, boy." The boy rushed over and took hold of Kruddup's elbow again, guiding him down the walkway to the dressing rooms, as the last and drunkest of the crowd found their way out of the Sportatorium.

With the boy's help, Kruddup led the investigator to the door at the far west end of the hall, labeled SECAF. It had been the code for the babyface dressing rooms in Southeast since the days of Earl, Sr. SECAF spelled FACES backward. For babyfaces.

Kayfabe.

Gabby stood watch outside the door.

"That's her, right there!" Junior's yelling caused him to double over with the pain in his ribcage before he could continue. Gabby was in street clothes but Junior recognized her right away.

"Mr. Kruddup, I would be happy to hear both yours and the lady's side of the story, after I speak with this Gorpp."

Kruddup lifted his head to reveal a face covered in sweat, flushed red and with a zigzagging vein standing out on his left temple. "You think you can keep us out of there, missy? Well, let me tell you something—" He gasped for a jagged breath and winced away the pain. "—this is my town, this is my building, I'm the one who put the sign on the goddamn door, so don't think you can stand there and tell the law—" Kruddup pointed incredulously at the rather nonchalant investigator still twirling the toothpick in his mouth. Then lost his breath.

"You're most welcome to come in," Gabby said, then turned and opened the door.

The cop went in first, followed by Junior with the usher keeping him on his feet, then Gabby. They found Gorpp face down on a wood table with a big wrestler-looking guy hunched over him, massaging his back.

Since when did Gorpp have a trainer? Junior thought. Was this just more of him trying to convey the trappings of a Champion, another flourish to go along with the robe and bowing to the audience? And who was this trainer with his back to them, seemingly oblivious of, or ambivalent about, the presence of the owner of Southeast Wrestling and a homicide investigator standing three feet behind him?

What in holy hell was going on?

"Mr. Gorpp?" the investigator said.

"That's me," Gorpp said. He turned to face the room, even as his trainer continued to give him a deep tissue massage interspersed with rhythmic chopping on his upper back.

"I'm here to speak to you about the disappearance of a Robert 'Buddy' Graham."

"Well, you came to the right place," Gorpp said.

The trainer turned around and smiled at Junior before turning to the investigator. "I'm Buddy Graham," he said.

Kruddup inhaled too fast in his rush to spew bile at Graham. That pokey rib felt like it had punctured his lung. He clutched his side and squeezed his eyes shut, hoping the pain would subside enough for him to scream at somebody. Anybody.

The investigator took the toothpick out of his mouth, furrowed his brow. "You're Buddy Graham?"

"That's me." Buddy handed over his Alabama driver's license for inspection.

"Sir, are you aware that your, uh, is it wife or—?"

"You mean, Sue?"

"Yes, that's the name. Sir, are you aware she filed a

missing person's report on you? She seems to be under the impression that Mr. Gorpp here may have had something to do with your disappearance."

"Well, Officer, I don't know how long you talked to Sue but she's under all sorts of impressions. Some of it's downright tinfoil hat stuff, if you know what I mean."

"Can you tell me your whereabouts these past several weeks since you were last seen in Mobile?"

"Sure. I was mostly shitfaced drunk in a hotel over in Biloxi, pissing away what little money this cheap sumbitch paid me." He sneered at Junior.

"And how do you come to be, uh, working with Mr. Gorpp?"

Gorpp sat up on the table.

"We just met tonight," Buddy said. "Before the match. Gorpp here told me he thought he might be in need of a massage after tangling with that Russian, and I was in need of a few bucks so we came to an arrangement pretty quick."

"A massage?" Kruddup gasped.

"That Dimitri gives some pretty hard bumps," Gorpp said. Then he smiled for a second time. No one saw Gabby standing in the back of the room, but she smiled too.

The investigator shook his head, tossed his toothpick in a rusty waste basket and walked out.

Case closed.

Junior gasped for breath, then managed one final bellow at his new whipping boy and seemingly the only loyal person left in his employ. "Take me to the goddamn hospital, boy!"

The usher slow-walked Junior out the back door to his Cadillac, helped him into the passenger's seat, then proceeded to drive him very slowly, peering over the steering wheel, to Providence Hospital.

Little did Junior know he would be attended by the same ER doc that treated Bear Claw Monroe.

CHAPTER 53

THE NEXT MORNING, Gorpp held a press conference in front of the United Nations headquarters in New York City. He stood behind a podium with a logo showing a moon revolving around Saturn with the words, "United Nations of Enceladus Territory Earth" encircling it. The nameplate on the podium read, "Gorpp, Supreme Ruler and Champion of Earth." It fit right in with the optics of the flags of nearly two-hundred nations behind him.

"I am Gorpp, your Supreme Ruler and three-time World Heavyweight Champion." He held up the belt and onlookers cheered their approval. A bank of TV cameras caught it all, including a guy selling Gorpp t-shirts from a converted pretzel stand on the corner. "Get your Gorpp souvenirs," he barked. "They're out of this world!"

UN Security kept their eye on things from a distance, but as long as the freak show stayed on the sidewalk, they figured less was more in terms of engagement.

"There's no law I know of saying funny looking wrestlers can't do their publicity stunts on the sidewalk if they want to. It's New York City. Am I right?" said one security guard to another.

"This isn't even the strangest thing I've seen this week," said the other with a laugh.

"What's this all about?" asked a Wall Street type who'd stumbled onto the scene.

One of the cameramen turned and said, "Some alien-looking wrestler guy says he's taking over the Earth is the gist."

"Can't be any worse than the peanut farmer," said Wall Street.

CHAPTER 54

Overalls had been monitoring a number of signals, radio waves and other transmissions from Earth since his unprecedented encounter with Gorpp just a few of his minutes ago. He briefed his superiors on the encounter, but they offered no response so he had to ponder its meaning on his own.

On one of his scans, he'd picked up Gorpp's appearance on the evening news with Marvin Castle, when he'd announced his intentions to take over the Earth on his own in front of the White House. Overalls transmitted the footage to Central Command. Predictably, they didn't respond.

He had been just about to transmit the appearance in front of the United Nations when he received a neural transmission that made it clear Central Command were watching it already and he should report immediately.

They summoned him in as soon as he arrived.

"You are to retrieve Gorpp at once," were their first words to him, spoken telepathically and as a chorus from the entire assembled leadership council for the invasion.

He turned to carry out his orders, but just as he did, the door opened and there stood Gorpp with his title belt around his waist.

"I am Gorpp!" he said aloud. "Supreme Ruler and Champion of Earth. I hereby order you to stand down your invasion."

The council winced and cringed at the vulgar auditory bombardment of spoken language. Gorpp didn't care. He had grown fond of the Earth custom of speaking aloud, and singing, and cries of joy, and wails of agony. He enjoyed hearing Steve Levey say, "and still Heavyweight Champion of the World… Goooorrrpppp!"

"We know who you are," boomed the collective voice of the council in his head. "We don't understand your actions."

Gorpp took a deep breath, and as he let it out, his shoulders slumped a little bit. He found subterfuge on this scale exhausting. And it felt like being asked to explain the punchline of a joke.

"After spending time with Earthlings, I have grown fond of them," Gorpp said.

The council didn't respond.

"I wish to take an Earthling to pair with," Gorpp added. "I don't want her to be harmed. I am here to do whatever I have to do to stop this invasion."

"The invasion has already been cancelled," came the voice of the council.

"It has?"

Gorpp hadn't heard the Earth expression, "don't look a gift horse in the mouth," but on his home world they had an expression with a similar meaning: "don't ask why the ice didn't crack."

He didn't want to ask but felt he had to know.

"Why has the invasion been cancelled?"

"According to our models, in the time it would take us to marshal our forces and put our assets in place for the invasion, this species will have caused their own Extinction Level Event. This is no longer an invasion. It is now a salvage operation."

"How long do they have?" Gorpp asked.

"Only a matter of days. At most, weeks."

Gorpp took another deep breath and felt himself drift in his mind. Roughly translated, he knew that meant that Gabby would be able to live out the most optimistic projection of her lifespan long before the extinction in Earth-time.

"Having already broken Rule Number One, you may return to Earth for their remaining time if you wish," the council said.

"I am Gorpp, Supreme Ruler and Champion of Earth!" Gorpp cried out, raising his belt over his head in unnecessary defiance.

The council members again squinted and contorted their faces in expressions of distaste.

CHAPTER 55

Several Earth-days later, Chip, the usher from the Sportatorium, helped Junior make the now arduous trip from his father's sprawling ranch-style house to his modest office in the industrial park.

Carol hadn't answered her phone since the double cross, and when he called her parents' house, her father made it clear he'd damn well better never call there again. He hadn't heard from the Russians. No surprise there. And if he ever laid eyes on that Judas referee again, he'd give him a reason to need an eye patch for real. But he knew he'd never see Mickey again. He'd surely ridden his new Jet Ski to a land far, far away from the Southeast territory by now. If he knew what was good for him.

Chip guided Junior up the metal stairs into the trailer. Junior jiggled the lock open and Chip helped him inside, then found the light switch inside the door.

"Where are my goddamn things?"

"Sir?"

"Where are my goddamn things, Chip?" Junior's eyes darted back and forth.

Chip had never set foot in his office before and didn't know how to respond.

"My things, Chip. My things! My file cabinets. The stacks of contracts I had on my hutch. My answering machine. Where are my goddamn things? I've been robbed!"

When the phone rang, it startled them both.

After it rang a second time, Junior hollered at Chip. "Answer the goddamn phone, will ya?"

Chip scurried over and answered, "Um, hello?"

"Hello, yes. This is Agent John Armstrong with the Internal Revenue Service Fraud Division. I need to speak to Mr. Earl Kruddup, Jr. Is he there?"

"Um—"

"It's a matter of some importance."

"Who is it on the goddamn phone?" Kruddup shouted, loud enough for Armstrong to hear.

Chip put a hand over the receiver and said, in a hushed voice, "It's the IRS. They say they need to talk to you right away, Mr. Kruddup."

Junior looked around at all the things missing from his office. They weren't things of value to a drug addict looking to score a quick fix. The things missing were his files. His records. His financial transactions.

Carol.

A final fuck you.

The twist of the knife. He could feel it in his side like a rib poking through the skin.

CHAPTER 56

GORPP's third reign as Champion was the one he will be most remembered for, and the one most written about in wrestling history books. He worked memorable programs, many of his own design, in every major territory on the US mainland. He wrestled in Puerto Rico, Alaska and Hawaii. It seemed as if distance and expense weren't even considerations. As Champion, Gorpp became an ambassador across the globe.

His program with the Red Devil in Mexico City is legendary in and of itself, for its violence, its poetry, and its plainspoken message of redemption.

The Mexican press billed it as a mask vs. mask type of match, in that if Gorpp lost, he agreed to be questioned by the Mexican government about his true origins. The Mexican media trumpeted that when Gorpp fell to the mighty Red Devil he would finally tell all about his extraterrestrial origins. If the Devil lost, he would unmask. To Mexican Lucha Libre fans, unmasking their idol bordered on the unthinkable. A violation. An insult on such a fundamental level. It couldn't be allowed to happen. Arena México had a capacity of 16,500 and there wasn't an empty seat in the house.

When Gorpp wrestled in Anchorage, Dimitri and his

family came from their hometown in Nikolaevsk to see him. Gorpp signed an autograph for Dimitri's nephew, who still used crutches from his accident, but would make a full recovery and be driving soon.

After the matches, Gorpp, Gabby, Dimitri and Alexi went to the Crooked Moose for beers and to talk about Dimitri's comeback. Because of the demand for Gorpp and the schedule he kept, he'd done more than a hundred and fifty main events across the globe in less than six months. But he was tired. He'd made his point. And he intended to hold up his end of the bargain with Dimitri. It turned out Alexi had been in touch with contacts in Moscow, and it looked like they would be able to stage the third and final showdown, again for the world title, this time in the USSR.

CHAPTER 57

GORPP AND GABBY sat in front of a warm fire. They wore matching bathrobes with Hotel Metropol Moscow insignias on them. Gorpp had learned that Gabby also drifted in her mind at times, the way he did. They were both looking into the flames in the large stone fireplace. The only sounds were the occasional crackle of a burning ember and the muted honking of car horns on the street below. Gabby turned her gaze out the window to a beautiful view of snow falling on downtown Moscow.

"What does your world look like?" she asked him.

"What do you mean?" Still looking into the fire.

She snapped out of her drift and looked at his profile. She could see the reflection of flames dancing in his large black eyes. "You know what I mean."

He came back too and looked at her. "I know what you mean but I'm not sure there are words in your language to translate what I would try to describe."

"The ice-covered moon of Enceladus, right? That's what you said on TV." She pushed his shoulder like a middle schooler trying to flirt in the lunchroom. "It even said it on the podium when you took over the United Nations. Remember? Aren't we like one of your territories now or something?"

"I'm from 'one of our territories' as you call it. I grew up on what Earthlings call Enceladus. I don't find the words in your language to describe what came before."

"Ok, well, describe Enceladus. Tell me something."

"The surface is fresh, clean ice. There are few more reflective bodies in this Solar System. And there are hundreds of geysers that shoot up out of the surface. The matter in those geysers make up some of the rings you see around Saturn."

"Is it cold?"

"On the surface it's about three-hundred and fifty degrees below freezing as you measure."

"How do you live in that?"

"We don't live on the surface."

Gorpp's gaze went to the sky outside their window where night had fallen on a snow-covered city. "Under the ice at the south pole of the moon there is a subsurface ocean. We live in the caverns beneath the water."

CHAPTER 58

Gorpp knew Overalls was trying to find him. Overalls had messaged him neuropathically, through his ship's console, through his implant, he'd even left a note at will-call at the Kansas City Memorial Auditorium when Gorpp wrestled in a steel cage match with Coyote Kiniski, and again at the O'Hare Airport Marriott in Chicago.

Gorpp didn't respond to any of it.

He couldn't think of anything Overalls could tell him that would be welcome news so, with the petulance of an Earthling, he avoided him, thereby delaying the consequences of whatever that message portended.

At least that's what he told himself.

Overalls almost cornered him coming out of Bullwackers Saloon halfway between Sturges and Spearfish in Whitewood, South Dakota, but Gorpp jumped on someone's Harley and sped away. In Havana, Cuba, Gorpp looked up to find his barista was Overalls. Gorpp dumped his cappuccino on him, caused a commotion and gave him the slip.

Sitting alone in a cold and drab locker room at the Moscow Coliseum, Gorpp sensed a presence. When he looked up, he saw Overalls, dressed the same as him, in his standard issue eggshell white jumpsuit.

"Is the invasion back on? Am I to be recalled? Why are you here?" Gorpp's eyes flicked back and forth and his pulse quickened.

Overalls didn't immediately respond.

"I'm dropping the title tonight. Do they not want that? Do they know that?"

"I want to wrestle," Overalls said.

Gorpp didn't respond.

"I want to do what you do," he said.

"That's why you're here? Earth is still safe?"

"That's why I'm here. And Earth is still safe, for the next few of our days anyway."

"And you want to wrestle?" Gorpp let out a short burst of laughter that sounded strange in his own ears.

"Very much," Overalls said.

"Ok," Gorpp slapped his knees. "How about tonight?"

"What do you mean?"

"I mean, I'm dropping the title tonight so I can get away from wrestling for a while, maybe a long while in Earth time. So, why don't you wrestle the match with Drozdov tonight, as me? Then you can work your way up to another run for the title. You know, pay your dues."

"Won't the Earthlings notice we don't look alike?" asked Overalls. The undercurrent of deception in wrestling would take some getting used to, even though he'd been watching as a fan for some time now, by Earth standards anyway, and learned from Gorpp.

"Not a chance," Gorpp said. "To them, we all look the same."

CHAPTER 59

It didn't work out as Gorpp had hoped.

"I'm one of the lucky ones. I've seen Gorpp wrestle live at ringside on a number of occasions. But I've never seen him look the way he did tonight," said Steve Levey, calling the match on tape for the Tampa Bay wrestling audience.

"Well, Steve, I've not only seen Gorpp wrestle, I've been in the ring with him. But I don't know if that makes *me* one of the lucky ones," said John White Eagle with a canned chuckle.

Levey joined in, selling for the legendary Florida worker trying to make the transition to color commentary.

"But seriously though. I don't know what happened in there tonight," White Eagle said. "If I didn't know better, I'd say that wasn't Gorpp."

"He did look sluggish, didn't he?" Levey said.

"More than sluggish, Steve," White Eagle said with a stern expression, direct to camera. "I've been a professional wrestler at the top of the sport for a long time now—"

"No question about that."

"—and I'm telling you, there was something wrong in that

ring tonight. Gorpp is a three-time World Champion. He's wrestled the world over. All the greats."

"Including you," Levey offered.

"Including me." White Eagle smiled at the camera. "But that wrestler in there tonight looked like he'd never stepped foot in a ring. He and Dimitri Drozdov had squared off twice before for the title. Gorpp knows Drozdov. But this, this imposter we saw tonight, it didn't seem like he knew Drozdov at all."

White Eagle was doing well making the transition from the ring to the announcing desk. And as long as he stayed on camera, he could still play to those rowdy female fans in Florida.

CHAPTER 60

Howie Shows didn't go so far as to suggest it had been an imposter in the ring in Moscow. His storyline was that for some, even the greats, they can grow old overnight. Shows wrote:

"No one can deny the mark Gorpp the Grappler has left on the world of professional wrestling. Love him or hate him, you simply cannot deny he has proved to be one of the greats. From his mystique to his near invincibility, well, it may be a cliché to say it but he has really been out of this world. It's natural to lament when we see a great Champion fall, but no one can stay atop the rough and tumble world of professional wrestling forever. On a snowy night in Moscow, we saw the end of a meteoric career. Gorpp will no doubt continue to be a fixture in popular culture and a curiosity to the viewing public for years to come. I, for one, think he did a lot of good for wrestling, bringing freshness and excitement and a new, younger audience to the sport."

He framed his piece with a collage of pictures highlighting Gorpp's career, including his press conference in front of the United Nations. In the crowd you could make out a young woman with a "Gorpp for President" shirt.

The headline on the cover read:

WHEN THE LIGHTS WENT OUT IN MOSCOW

The picture showed a confused and off-balance Gorpp. Something wrestling fans had never seen before.

CHAPTER 61

THE REAL GORPP had gotten very comfortable in the passenger seat of Gabby's Mustang. They tried to keep a low profile while enjoying an extended road trip across North America. They took the Alcan Highway from Vancouver all the way to Anchor Point, Alaska. Legend has it that when Captain James Cook discovered the place, he lost his anchor, hence the name. Though the Athabaskans had been calling it Dena'ina long before Captain Cook came along.

The trip put almost 2,500 more miles on Gabby's Mustang. She didn't know if the car would make it, but Gorpp turned out to be very handy at tinkering when it got temperamental. Still, in all, she thought they might need to swap the old Mustang for a truck to make the return trip. The two were sitting on a log gazing out at Cook Inlet when Gorpp lurched to attention, jumped up and started looking around.

"What are you doing?" Gabby said. "We're not fugitives. Relax."

He ignored her and scanned the hillsides in each direction. He turned back around to find Overalls standing right next to Gabby.

Gorpp leapt to put himself between Gabby and what the

primal part of his brain signaled as danger. But he stopped himself. Overalls didn't represent a threat. His mind had conflated danger with surprise. Overalls didn't flinch. He knew Gorpp wouldn't hurt him, and he'd been in the ring with mean, hairy, stinking human wrestlers leaping at him—and much worse—for months.

"Why are you here?"

"I have information."

Overalls hadn't tried to send him a message, or contact him in any way. Instead, he'd tracked him down in Alaska to talk to him face-to-face. To share information he thought Gorpp should have.

"What is it?"

"When you changed course and went to Florida to pursue your quest, the shipment you failed to deliver included your dose of the vaccine against Poison Ocean Syndrome. Your prognosis is not favorable."

"How much time do I have?"

"Probably only a few days."

"Our days or Earth days?"

"Our days."

Gorpp considered then smiled and looked at Gabby. "We'll grow old together," he said.

A tear welled in her eye. She wiped it away and put her hand on his arm.

"There is more," Overalls said.

They both turned to look at him.

"I have failed to adapt."

Gorpp and Gabby didn't respond.

"I have failed to adapt to Earth, to wrestling, to the filth and noise and deception of this world. When I look at you, I see harmony. When I watched your wrestling career, I saw glory. With me in your place, I have found none of that, and I wish to return."

Unbeknownst to any of them, an environmental activist

named Seth Rolley watched them from the cliff above. He couldn't really hear their conversation, but being a wrestling fan, he knew who Gorpp and Firefly were. He'd been taking pictures of damage caused by oil exploration with a telephoto lens when he spotted them. He developed the pictures in his bathroom converted to a darkroom, and sold them to the *Star Globe*. He used the money to print flyers in opposition to oil drilling in Cook Inlet.

For reasons unknown, the pictures were never printed.

On their last night at the Captain Cook State Recreation Area, Overalls retired to his vessel while Gorpp and Gabby stared, mesmerized, into a fire they'd built. Gorpp broke a long silence filled by nothing but the wind.

"Regret is an uncomfortable emotion," he said.

"What do you regret?"

"That Dimitri will know we were nearby and didn't inquire about the wellbeing of his nephew."

Gabby put her hand on his shoulder and gave a squeeze.

"Do you find that deception can ease the discomfort of regret?" Gorpp asked.

"What are you thinking?"

"I could tell Dimitri we weren't really in Alaska. That it was a work."

"So, your idea is to lie to him to feel better about not checking on his nephew?"

Gorpp didn't respond.

"You know," Gabby said, "sometimes your feelings are uncomfortable, but you have to feel them anyway."

For a long time neither of them spoke again. Then, Gorpp said, "Your vehicle isn't well-suited to make the return trip to Tampa. But we no longer need it." He motioned behind him to where Overalls had tucked his vessel into the bushes.

"What do you propose we do with it? My daddy got me that car." She crinkled her brow, but Gorpp picked up more playfulness than sentimentality in her tone.

"I have a solution" Gorpp said.

Gabby looked at him with a smile. "You want to leave it for Dimitri's nephew, don't you?"

He met her gaze. It pleased him how in synch their thinking could be without verbal communication. "Yes," he said.

"Ok," she said. "But what am I supposed to drive?"

"I have a solution for that too."

CHAPTER 62

ERNIE AND BOBBY were back in a corner booth at the Cuban place in Ybor City. Gorpp and Gabby, who'd gotten a quick lift back from Overalls, sat across from them. They kept their heads down. The owner assured Ernie news wouldn't get out of a Gorpp sighting in his place. Gorpp wore a hoody and his Ray-Bans just in case.

Gorpp thumbed through a stack of back issues of *World Wrestling Digest* Ernie had brought with him. It was worse even than Overalls had let on. After the disaster with Dimitri, things had only gone downhill. He'd lost successive matches after losing the title. He'd become a laughing stock.

"The real question isn't where is he from, it's when is he going back?" quipped a comedian on *The Tonight Show*.

After the mainstream media had their fun mocking and taunting the mighty Gorpp on his downfall, Howie Shows summed it up this way:

"This isn't just a fall from the top of the wrestling world but a fall from grace. Gorpp used to demand respect even from the skeptics and detractors because he couldn't be beat in the squared circle. Strangely, this stranger brought a new credibility to our beloved wrestling. He brought a new generation of fans, and ushered in a kind of renaissance for the sport. He claimed to be here to take over not just wrestling but planet Earth. Well, like it has to so many greats before him, the wrestling business and life here on Earth have beaten this Champion down, reduced him to a pathetic caricature of his former self. It's the oft asked question: why didn't he walk away, if not before the Drozdov match in Moscow, then at least after? If he'd bowed and left the stage when he was beaten by a competitor worthy of holding the title—like Dimitri Drozdov—then he would have lost no face with wrestling fans. But sadly, that question is all we're left with now. Why? Why does he go on digging the grave of his once otherworldly reputation deeper and deeper?"

Gorpp looked up to find they were watching him read. Gabby was leaning into him and reading it too. "Whew," she said. "That's some strong medicine." In addition to the damage control they would need to do for Gorpp, she couldn't help but think, after Bear Claw Monroe and Nat Pfeifer read about how Dimitri was "worthy of holding the title," they would cancel their subscriptions.

"Here's what we're thinking—" Ernie started.

"—We actually have the angle worked out," Gabby said.

Bobby smiled at her. It seemed like a million years ago when he'd found her waiting tables at the bar by the Armory. Gorpp was a lucky bastard.

Ernie looked at Bobby and then back at Gabby. "Let's hear it, sweetheart."

CHAPTER 63

THE *STAR GLOBE* moved lots of copy. They broke the story of Gorpp's return with this headline:

FIGHT FOR MOON OF SATURN COULD DECIDE FATE OF EARTH

The cover photo—exclusive to the *Star Globe*—showed Gorpp and Overalls locked in hand-to-hand combat on a frozen tundra. The caption claimed it was the ice surface of Enceladus but Gabby had actually taken the pictures of Gorpp and Overalls at the North Pole. Earthlings would never know the difference. The *Star Globe's* version of the story implied that in addition to the good twin (Gorpp) and the evil twin (Overalls) battling for the moon of Enceladus, Earth and beyond, there was also a rivalry for the affections of the lovely Firefly. *Star Globe* readers mostly took it at face value.

Howie Shows told a different story to his audience. His headline:

WRESTLING'S GREATEST MYSTERY – SOLVED!

"I knew that wasn't him!" John White Eagle told the *Digest*. "I knew it the night I saw him wrestle in Moscow. The night he lost the title. I guarantee you, that's when the twin stepped in."

In Howie's version, Overalls had indeed kidnapped Gorpp and assumed his identity to sabotage his career and ruin his reputation. To take away his legacy just for the sake of mean spiritedness. In the letters section, fans would soon be demanding a brother against brother showdown.

Ernie billed it as, "the match for Gorpp's good name." It wasn't his most inspired slogan—he was old and tired—but the angle proved irresistible. He most certainly could have made more money in a larger market, but Gorpp and Overalls didn't care, so Ernie staged the match at Pensacola Civic Arena, mainly to send a message to Earl Kruddup, Jr.

CHAPTER 64

STEVE LEVEY GOT the festivities underway.

"Ladies and gentlemen, good evening. Heavyweight Championship Wrestling from Florida is proud to be here in the Pensacola Civic Arena to present the return of former three-time World Heavyweight Champion, hailing from parts unknown, Goooorrppp!"

Gorpp appeared in his silk robe and gleaming black eyes to a smattering of applause, but the crowd seemed on edge, not yet committed to a partisan stance on the battle of the spacemen brothers.

Firefly appeared by Gorpp's side in an elaborate ensemble of her own, including skintight purple and orange tights with rhinestones and makeup to match. Whether she was his valet, his manager or his paramour was the subject of both murmured debate in the arena and more letters to the *Digest*, some too racy to print. They made their way to the ring to his usual "Flying Saucers Rock-n-Roll" theme song with the occasional subdued wave to a young fan.

Gorpp had just entered the ring when Overalls appeared, seemingly from out of nowhere, and attacked him from behind. No introductions, no ring walk. This was not the befuddled, bumbling and cowardly buffoon wrestling fans had been duped by these past months. This was like watching a crocodile leap from under the water to surprise and take down a zebra.

Firefly had been knocked to her knees in the initial burst of violence when Overalls overwhelmed Gorpp. Many in the crowd stood to get the best view they could. She appeared confused. They could see her tense to join the fray but then they followed her eyes and saw what she must be seeing. You couldn't tell them apart. As fast as they were moving, a whirring tangle of limbs, she didn't know which one to help and which to hinder.

At one point, she got hit in the back of the head by a misguided kick that sent her tumbling out of the ring. As Firefly climbed to her hands and knees, one of the brothers prepared to perform Gorpp's trademark flying saucer. He became a blur of white, then the other one sailed over the top rope and over the heads of the first twenty-six rows of the arena. He crashed into a rowdy group of charter fishermen who didn't mind taking a bump for the sake of the show. The combatant ejected from the ring didn't appear injured, or even fazed, and had nothing but sneers and angry words for the fans around him as he made his way back, so folks pretty much figured this was the evil twin.

Some of the local rowdies looked on the verge of making it difficult for Overalls to get back to the ring, but when the humans felt his presence and saw him close up, it took the starch out of them pretty quick.

Overalls slid back into the ring ahead of the referee's ten count and they squared off again. As soon they clenched, it again became difficult to tell them apart. Gorpp almost immediately got Overalls in another flying saucer. This time he kept spinning until just watching them was dizzying.

When Gorpp let Overalls go, he was spinning so fast, and feeling so dizzy himself, he lost his balance. Instead of Overalls sailing up in an arc over the crowd he shot out straight from Gorpp's shoulders, cracked his head on the steel post behind the turnbuckle and crashed into the first row.

Then he disappeared.

The ref started counting but then stopped when he realized he couldn't see the wrestler who'd just flown from the ring, who surely must be in need of medical attention. The crowd looked around, and so did Gorpp and Firefly.

Steve Levey grabbed the microphone and made an announcement over the PA. "Please turn on the house lights. Thank you."

The house lights lit up the arena. Beer cans, cigarette butts and popcorn littered the aisles. But there was no sign of Overalls. Gorpp was leaning over the ropes, peering out into the crowd when Overalls appeared behind him. Blood gushed from a huge gash across his forehead and bright red stains soaked his white uniform. He raised a steel chair over his head and started toward Gorpp. The crowd tried to warn him but he ended up turning just in time for Overalls to smash the chair over his head, as they'd planned.

Gorpp crumpled to his knees on the canvass, and bowed his bleeding head. Overalls raised the chair over his head again, and appeared ready to deliver a potentially fatal blow, when Firefly leapt from the top turnbuckle, hitting him with her signature crossbody block before he could bring the chair down on Gorpp's prone form. He ended up landing on top of the chair with Firefly crashing down on top of him. When she leapt up to tend to Gorpp, Overalls didn't move and the referee called for the bell.

Gorpp was still on the mat when the referee raised his hand to cheers from the crowd. He'd gotten over with the angle even though they were hesitant at first.

"John, it's not clear if they're awarding the match to Gorpp on a count out or a disqualification, but I suppose at the end of the day, a win is a win. Isn't that right?"

"That's right," White Eagle said. "This was a grudge match. Brother against brother. I'll tell you what else, Steve. I think Firefly may well have saved Gorpp's life."

Howie latched on to the fraternal angle too. He got into some hot water for having so much blood on the cover of the *Digest*. It was a bit much, especially for the grocery chains and drug stores in the Bible Belt. In addition to the gory photo, his headline, in dripping red letters simply read:

BLOOD BROTHERS

Overalls had really resisted the juicing angle. Just the germs on the ring mat gave him the creeps, so bleeding all over each other was the last thing he wanted to do. But he'd played his part perfectly. The angle went over big time. As soon as it was done and he got cleaned up, he wanted to get back to Central Command and be done with humans once and for all.

CHAPTER 65

Gorpp and Firefly were back.

The owners at the 1979 annual meeting in Lake Tahoe decided there was no reason to put the belt on Gorpp for a fourth time. Dimitri was a credible Champion who played ball and made the local babyfaces look good, even in defeat. He got plenty of heat with his Russian heel schtick, and this way they figured they could make twice as much keeping Dimitri on the road and getting Gorpp back out there too as a featured attraction. He was so famous he didn't need the title to sell tickets.

Ernie worried he'd catch it hot for having both the World Champion and the main draw in wrestling back in his stable, but with both of them regularly visiting the territories, enough money came in to keep the grumbling to a minimum.

Overalls sent Gorpp a message. He felt bad that he hadn't been able to return the title belt when he went back to Central Command. Gorpp assured him he didn't miss it. He was enjoying a more flexible schedule.

"I can't resist pointing out that having those feelings in the first place is very human of you," Gorpp said.

Overalls didn't respond.

CHAPTER 66

Bobby leaned his head out of the office and called out so they could hear him at the ring. "Hey, Ernie. It's John White Eagle on the phone."

"Tell him I'm—" Ernie cut himself off and started hobbling to the office, grumbling. He grabbed the phone from Bobby and barked into it. "Johnny, what the hell do you want? I'm trying to run a wrestling business here—"

"That's what I'm calling about, Mr. Cantrell. I'll cut right to the chase. I think there's money to be made with Firefly and I'd like to give her a push down here in Miami. See if we can set up an angle that leads to Calvin putting the women's belt on her."

Earnie plopped himself down in his chair, took his cigarettes from his shirt pocket and lit one up with the lighter on his desk. The fan swirled the smoke around and lifted a few papers from the desk. In all these years in the business, he'd never given serious thought to the notion there was real money to be made with the women, but Gabby was something special. She had the look, the toughness and the aerial athleticism that made her exciting to watch. The gimmick worked. All of that, combined with her association with Gorpp, had put her in a unique position.

Nobody paid too much mind, but Hank Frizzel up in Charlotte had the women's title on a gal they were calling the next Mildred Burke.

Karla Becker coached wrestling at Faith Women's College in southern Georgia. In 1972, a local news anchor interviewed Karla about a professional wrestling card in Valdosta.

"I'm here in the gymnasium at Faith Women's College," said Timothy Reid, the anchor. "As you can see and hear, there is wrestling going on behind me. What's unusual is, it's women wrestling. I'm joined by Karla Becker. She coaches the women's wrestling team here at Faith. Coach Becker, what I see here behind us looks like something that could take place in the Olympics. I don't see any eye gouging or name calling, no steel chairs. As you may know, there is so-called 'professional' wrestling happening this weekend in Valdosta. My question to you: is professional wrestling real?"

Becker gave him a half smile. And that much only because they were on TV. She thought for a second, standing with her hands on her hips in a broad wrestler's stance.

"Let me put it to you this way, Mr. Reid. It's every bit as real as you should want it to be."

Reid crinkled his brow. He didn't know what to make of that answer. "Will you be there for the matches?"

"We have a meet in Donaldsonville that same night."

They went on like that for a while. The interview ended when Karla offered to show Reid a few holds but he begged off. By the time it was over, Reid was emasculated and the town had a new hero. A draft Karla Becker campaign got started up to get her into the professional ranks. People actually stood out in front of supermarkets with clipboards and petitions. The townspeople sent those petitions to Sam Calvin and soon enough, Karla was blazing a trail to the women's title.

Karla's matches were works, but she'd already beaten back more than one double cross attempt in the ring in her five years as Champion. The acrobatic Firefly was the first contender for Becker's title that anyone thought had a chance in several years.

WOMEN'S TITLE MATCH UPSTAGED BY BEAR CLAW'S REVENGE

That was Howie's headline.

The angle had started on a local Charlotte TV taping of Frizzel's weekly studio show where they hyped the big matches at the Coliseum. Coach Becker, as they called the champ, came out in her usual gym shorts and sweatshirt that looked like it was for a college athletic program but, if you looked closely, said, "Women's World Wrestling Champion." She had a whistle around her neck and the title belt around her waist.

"I'm here today with a message for Firefly, or *the* Firefly, or whatever she calls herself. She's been out there buzzing around, saying she wants a shot at my world title. But I saw what she did in the so-called 'blood brothers' match. She interfered. Now, I come from collegiate wrestling where we wrestle with honor and we follow the rules. If Firefly wants to step into the ring with me, I'm going to stipulate that I can have someone in my corner who has my back if she tries any illegal tactics. That is my one condition, Firefly. Take it or leave it."

"Well, ladies and gentlemen," said the Charlotte announcer, Gil Breckenridge, "there you have it, straight from Coach Karla Becker, the undisputed Women's Champion. She's thrown the gauntlet down. We'll have to wait and see what Firefly has to say about that."

The next day, they taped a promo with Firefly standing on East Kennedy Boulevard in front of City Hall in Tampa.

"Greetings from sunny Florida," she said with a smile. "I'm standing here in front of City Hall because this is where they're going to have my parade, right here on Kennedy Boulevard, when I bring the women's world title home to Florida. Coach Becker, you bring along anyone you want. And so will I." With that, she leapt up onto the wall behind her and appeared to be scaling it when they cut away.

Frizzel's studio show opened with a *breaking news* segment where his two hosts announced they'd just received word that Women's Champion Karla Becker would be seconded by none other than men's World Champion Dimitri Drozdov.

"We're not aware of any previous ties between the two champions, are we?"

"We are not. But we do know about the history between Drozdov and Firefly's, shall we say, significant other?"

"Well, I'll tell you this. This women's match was already generating more interest than any I can remember, and I've been doing this a long time."

"And it's getting more interesting by the minute, isn't it?"

Everyone assumed Firefly would have Gorpp in her corner. Who else would it be? When the night of the match arrived, she still hadn't made an announcement.

As the challenger, Firefly came out first. Alone. The announcers made note of it but didn't linger on the topic. She got a warm welcome in Charlotte. Becker came out with Dimitri to scattered applause and boos. In five years, Coach Becker had enjoyed periods of popularity. She was always respected, but her lack of quality competition and resulting dominance had left the local crowd fatigued and open to the promise of a new Champion. Frizzel knew it. He worked out with Becker that the Drozdov-Monroe interference would spare her losing in a clean finish, but she would lose the title on a disqualification. That wasn't really a thing, but the crowd went along with it. And it set up a rematch. Coach Becker would complain bitterly and convincingly that she shouldn't have lost her title on what she called a "DQ," but the fact was Firefly had the title belt with her back in the Sunshine State, and the angle lived on.

The DQ ended up being talked about more than the world title changing hands.

The match had been a great contrast between Coach Becker's scientific approach, where she tried to keep her opponent on the mat, and Firefly's aerial acrobatics and her increasingly well-known finisher, the cross body block off the top rope. It had been a seesaw battle for going on thirty minutes. Coach Becker was older and not used to being tested. She appeared to be more fatigued than Firefly. After languishing in a leglock from Becker, Firefly broke free and suddenly had a burst of energy. While Becker started getting up off the mat, Firefly climbed the ropes and prepared to leap when, from behind her, Dimitri grabbed her ankle and pulled her down. On the way, she fell awkwardly on her knee and rolled back and forth in pain on the floor outside the ring.

When the referee saw she couldn't continue, he ruled Firefly the winner by disqualification, and awarded her the title belt. Dimitri started showering the ref with obscenities, in English and in Russian. He threatened to get into the ring and take the belt back himself if the referee didn't. When he started to climb up on the ring apron, Bear Claw Monroe came storming from the back of the stands with his long beard and bearskin vest, looking like a caveman. He grabbed hold of Dimitri from behind, pulled him down onto the floor of the coliseum and furiously and repeatedly stomped on him with his big boots until the Champion was a bloody mess on the floor. Then he applied his infamous "bear claw."

Dimitri issued the following statement the next day to *World Wrestling Digest*. Though, in truth, Ernie wrote it and Dimitri never even knew exactly what it said.

From the desk of the Heavyweight Champion of the World: "I have filed a formal complaint with the North

Carolina Athletic Commission..." (he hadn't) "and the sanctioning body, Heavyweight Championship Wrestling..." (also hadn't) "to dispute both the disqualification my actions are being blamed for, and the resulting title change. Given the injuries caused by Firefly's aerial assault of a non-combatant in a prior match, as Coach Becker was wary of from the start, when I saw her mount the ropes and prepare to jump, I could tell Coach Becker was vulnerable. I didn't intend to cause harm to Firefly or cause the match to end. I was just trying to prevent unnecessary injury to Coach Becker. My attorneys..." (he had none) "are also preparing a case against Robert 'Bear Claw' Monroe for his unprovoked attack."

Nobody bought any of it but that didn't matter. It was just Dimitri being the heel American fans were comfortable with him being. People were excited about Firefly as Champion and they weren't too concerned with all the details of how it came about.

CHAPTER 67

"Hey, Ernie. The phone!" Bobby yelled from the office.

"What's with you and the goddamn phone all the time?" Ernie yelled back at him, then went back to working on a hip roll with Tommy "The Man" Branson.

"It's Sam Calvin."

Ernie looked like he'd gotten the wind knocked out of him. "Tommy," he said. "You wanna work your way up the card, you gotta get the basic stuff down. It's gotta be so engrained—" he pointed at his temple "—that it's second nature. You hear me, Tommy? You really hear me?" Tommy had just turned twenty-three-years-old. To Ernie, he seemed more like thirteen.

"I hear you, Mr. Cantrell. I hear you cloud and rear. I mean, loud and clear."

"Jesus Christ." Ernie made his way, hobbling at some clip toward the office, a cigarette in hand and muttering under his breath.

The boys in the locker room called Tommy "Cloud and Rear" for months after that.

Ernie shooed Bobby out of the cramped office and slammed the door shut. "Sam? I'm working here, but I figure you wouldn't be calling if it wasn't important, so tell me what it is that's so goddamn important."

"Ernie, I got owners calling me, they're going through the fucking roof. I couldn't believe it at the owners' meeting when nobody busted your balls over having the goddamn title and your spaceman act in the Florida territory. But—"

"Hold on a second, Sam. You're calling to tell me other owners are whining like babies because I'm running my business better than they are?"

"Hold on, Ernie—"

"What, cause I got better talent? Better angles? It's my fault somehow that people want the product I'm selling more than the ones they're selling? Somebody's gotta lead the pack, right?"

"Ernie, slow down. You haven't even let me get to the reason I'm calling."

Ernie lit and took a drag on a cigarette with a trembling and sun-spotted hand. He waited.

"The reason I'm calling," Calvin said. "Ernie, you can't have the Women's Champion too. You just—"

"Oh, give it a fucking rest, Sam! Seriously. Who's squawking about this anyway?"

"Well, Kruddup, for one, and—"

"Kruddup? That little peckerwood. You think I give a rat's ass what Earl's idiot son thinks of me? I do not."

"Ernie, you still didn't let me finish. He's sore about Dimitri leaving—"

"Tough shit," Ernie said. "I didn't like it when Dimitri and Alexi left here either, but you didn't hear me bitching about it. Hell, you may not have been around long enough to remember Buddy Graham was down here in the Florida territory before he went up to Southeast back in Earl Senior's day."

"He says your ladies' champ there punctured his lung

with her cross body block. I wouldn't be surprised if he filed a lawsuit."

"From what I hear, Junior's gonna be too busy defending himself against tax evasion charges to be suing anybody himself. But listen, Sam, if this is as close as you've got to anything serious to talk about, then I've gotta get back to work. I've got a kid out here who looks like he should be mowing lawns or delivering newspapers to me. He doesn't know a hip roll from a jellyroll. And he thinks he should be the top of the card. Just like they all do, right? Anyway, listen, you're a sweetheart to try to look out for Earl's idiot son. You've done your due diligence. Now I'm getting back to work."

Ernie hung up the phone, put out his cigarette, and marched in his staggered gait back out to the ring where he belonged. "That's not right. Stop! That's not right," he barked at Tommy. Ernie turned, made eye contact with Bobby, and scowled at him. "No more goddamn phone calls," he said. "I don't care if it's the Father, the Son and the Holy Spirit on a goddamn party line. No more calls."

That evening, when Ernie went to buy cigarettes at a small market off Howard Avenue, he got a twenty-five-cent Florida postcard with a girl in a bikini on it. The next morning, before Bobby got there, Ernie put a stamp on it, wrote the St. Louis headquarters address on it, and this note:

"Sam, greetings from sunny Florida. The young lady on the other side of this card is almost as tan as you and a whole lot prettier. Your pal, Ernie." He was walking back from mailing the card, smoking a cigarette, when he met up with Bobby coming from the other direction. They gave each other a nod good morning and Ernie unlocked the Armory.

"I just got one question," Bobby said.

Ernie knew he'd figure out to ask.

"How did they get Dimitri to go along with it?"

"How do you think?" Ernie said to his protégé.

"It was Dimitri's idea," he said, almost like he was having a lucid dream.

"When Bear Claw Monroe got home to St. Paul he had a crate of Russian vodka on his doorstep. Dimitri told me he knew he couldn't make it right, what he'd done, but he could at least apologize, get him a payday and maybe a chance to save face."

CHAPTER 68

CHIP DROVE Junior out to Sue's place. He still had to help him out of the car, but once he was up, he could move at a decent clip with his cane.

"You stay with the car," Junior told him and started his way toward the old mobile home. Kudzu, green mold and vines crawled up the sides. A hungry looking dog peered out from underneath and growled, but Junior didn't pay it any mind. He noticed a neighbor sitting on their porch watching him. He supposed it wasn't every day a big Cadillac with a chauffeur pulled up to Sue's place. Junior decided not to risk the rickety steps and just stood at the bottom and used his cane to tap on the door. There were no sounds from inside. A beat up F150 sat parked in the drive but he couldn't tell if it still ran. He tapped a little louder with his cane and the muffled sounds of a small dog could be heard yipping inside. Junior made eye contact with the staring neighbor.

"You know if she's home?" he hollered.

The neighbor continued staring right at him as if he hadn't spoken.

Junior turned back to the door and this time he wacked

his cane on it hard enough to dent the tin with each strike. Now, the yipping really picked up. And the dog beneath the trailer added a few barks of its own. He considered wandering around back but his side hurt and he didn't like the neighbor staring at him. He started back to the car. Chip was sitting in the driver's seat pointing back at the trailer. Junior turned just in time to see a curtain that had been pulled to the side fall back into place. He made his way back to the door.

"Sue, it's Earl Kruddup, Jr. We need to talk, and I'm not leaving here until we do."

No response. Junior turned his back to the trailer and sat down on those rickety steps. After a few minutes, he hollered at Chip.

"Go pick us up some gizzards and fried pickles from Hart's. And get some chicken and rolls too. Enough for three. Go on, I'm hungry!"

Chip blazed out of the dirt driveway fast enough to leave a dust cloud in his wake.

"And some cobbler!" Junior hollered, but Chip didn't hear him.

He figured it should take him about forty-five minutes, but an hour later he was still sitting in the baking sun, sweat matting his shirt to his skin. He hadn't even noticed Sue had cracked the door until her yippy little dog squeezed through and started sniffing his back from the step above where he was sitting. Junior had the wherewithal to turn around real slow like.

"Hey there, pup," he said to the mangy little mongrel. He could see the door was cracked and looked up slowly to see a few inches of Sue's light blue terrycloth bathrobe, then her pained face.

"You look hot," she said. "You wanna come in for some sweet tea?"

"Thank you kindly," Junior said, slowly getting to his feet. "That would be real nice." He grabbed a hold of the handrail and eased his weary body up the creaky stairs and into Sue's trailer.

It took his eyes a minute to adjust to the dim light inside. Dirty coffee cups obscured the view of a soap on a small black-and-white TV on the kitchen counter. Despite her bathrobe and yellowing skin from the cigarettes she chain-smoked, Sue was still an attractive, if deeply troubled, woman.

"Have a seat," she said, motioning to a chair piled with dirty laundry. Junior leaned on his cane and moved the pile of clothes with his other hand, then sat. "You look like shit, Junior. I guess it's true that little girl roughed you up pretty good, huh? The one that's been hanging around with the, you know—"

"Could I get that tea?" Junior asked.

Sue headed for the refrigerator and somehow managed to break ice out of the tray from the freezer, pour the tea, and hand it to him without ever putting her cigarette down. He looked at the glass that didn't appear to have been washed, but took a deep gulp of the tea anyway.

"Thank you," he said. "That's good."

Sue stood staring at him and took another drag on her cigarette.

"Have you had lunch?" Junior asked. "I've got some chicken and gizzards coming from Hart's."

"What do you want, Junior?" Sue tapped the ashes of her cigarette onto the floor. It was a wonder the place hadn't burned down.

"Have you seen Buddy?"

"What are you, a marriage counselor now?"

"I didn't realize you were—"

"I'm going to ask you one more time, Junior. I didn't invite you over here. I don't want your chicken and gizzards. I don't need to talk to anybody about my old man. Now, what do you want with me?"

"I need to know what happened the night Buddy disappeared. You saw something. I can see it in your eyes, in the way you're living, Sue. Something happened that scared the daylights out of you. Now, what was it?"

Sue took another drag on her cigarette, then snuffed it out in an overfull ceramic ashtray. She pulled her robe tight around her, pulled back the curtain just a tad and looked out, then she straightened her posture and braced her hands on the edge of the counter.

"Junior, I'm gonna tell you this one time. I'm not gonna repeat it. And when I'm done I want you and your gizzards and your chauffeur to get the hell off my property and never come back. We clear?"

He wanted to protest but he didn't. "We're clear."

She looked toward the window even though she couldn't see out. "It was, I don't know, a little after two. We were there to close up the Port City Pub that night and they close at two, so, maybe fifteen minutes after that, we pull up in the drive out front. I was driving my truck 'cause Buddy was never in any shape to drive by the time we got home from a bar. I remember I fell coming up the front steps, but we were both laughing about something, and when I fell we both just laughed harder. I skinned up my hip pretty good but I didn't even know that until the next day." She looked again toward the closed curtain.

Junior took another tentative sip of tea from the grimy glass.

"He helped me up, you know. And I was looking for my damn keys. I'd just had 'em but they weren't in my purse. I climbed back down the stairs and started looking for 'em where I'd fallen, but it was dark and the porch light had blown out." Sue shivered, and when she spoke next there was a hitch in her voice, like she may start crying. "I hollered for

Buddy to go back and see if I'd left 'em in the truck." She paused and took a few breaths. "He didn't answer. Then, I got this real cold feeling all of a sudden, even though it was warm and humid that night. I called for him again, loud this time. The sound of my own voice scared me. I was scrabbling around with my hand in the dark, huntin' for my keys, and calling out for Buddy. Then, under the stairs, I felt the keys, grabbed 'em and headed back up the steps so I could turn a light on inside and see if I could figure out what was going on. When I put the key in the lock, I heard something behind me. I turned. I turned and, Junior, I swear to God Almighty, I saw that alien. The real one that you had Buddy pretending to be. He looked at me with those cold, black eyes and then he was gone. And so was Buddy."

She took a few ragged breaths, then started looking for a pack of cigarettes.

Junior took another small sip of tea and set the glass down on the coffee table, on top of a stack of old TV guides.

"That's what I saw. That's all I know. And that's all I'm gonna say about it. I don't ever even want to think about it again." She took a deep drag on her cigarette and looked at the filthy brown shag rug.

"Now that you know Buddy is ok, that he was working with—"

"Don't say that name in my house."

"Now that you know they were working together when Buddy came back. Do you think they planned it together from the start? Sue, that's what I'm trying to figure out. Because I think they did. I think they were both playing us from the very beginning. Setting us up for a fall. And look at us now. Look at us."

"Get out," she said. She motioned to the door with the hand holding her cigarette.

Junior stood, got his cane and headed for the door. As he

made his way carefully down the steps, she spoke from behind him.

"And don't come back," she said, then closed the door.

Junior got to the bottom of the steps and realized goddamn Chip still wasn't back, so he sat down and started sweating again.

CHAPTER 69

Junior sat there until the sun started to sink into the western horizon. Good thing he'd had some of Sue's tea. He already felt a bit parched. He couldn't knock on that door again. The neighbor had at least gone inside. He passed the time swatting at gnats and mosquitoes, and daydreaming about beating Chip senseless with his cane, and then eating all the gizzards and chicken and cobbler himself. And then taking a piss.

It must have been getting on to six o'clock when a white Ford sedan pulled up in the drive. A frumpy fellow with glasses and greasy hair got out of the car.

"You Mr. Earl Kruddup?"

"Who's asking?"

"My name is Benjamin Flowers. I'm an agent with the Internal Revenue Service. Sir, I'd like you to come with me."

"I'm waiting on my, my chauffeur. He's bringing me lunch," Junior said, doubtfully, as he looked at the sun going down.

"Sir, Mr. Tadwell was relieved of the keys to your vehicle at a Hart's Fried Chicken on South Wilson Avenue earlier today." He gave that a minute to sink in. "I'm going to need you to come with me."

Flowers wiped beads of sweat from his forehead and looked at the window of Sue's trailer just as the curtain dropped back into place.

CHAPTER 70

ERNIE PUT money away during the Gorpp era like he'd never even heard of, much less seen before. The combination of crossover fan appeal, Gorpp's inhuman travel schedule, and his disinterest in money for the most part had put Ernie in a comfortable position to retire.

He was drinking a beer and smoking a cigar at noon, sitting at an outdoor bar in Key West called Hemingway's Hideaway. The breeze swirled around him, like the old oscillating fan in his office at the Armory had for all those years. He had had as good a run as anybody, and he went out on top and with a once in a lifetime payout.

That was good enough for Ernie.

He didn't need a retirement party, a big article in the *Digest* or a plaque from Sam Calvin. This cold beer, the smell of coconut suntan oil on the skin of the pretty girls that walked by, his shoulders free of the weight of payrolls and politics and pricks in the business—that was more than enough. He was ready to replace it all with a gentle breeze, a great view and a little peace of mind.

He was ready to cash out.

"Sir," said the young bartender, putting a phone down in front of him. "You have a call."

"What are you, jerking my chain?" Ernie looked around. "Is this that show where they play practical jokes on people with a hidden camera rolling in the bushes somewhere? Seriously. I'm just trying to relax here, so—"

"You're Mr. Cantrell, right?"

"Yes."

"You have a call, sir. They said it was important."

"I swear to God," Ernie said. "This is too much. How far do I have to go? The Outback?"

The waiter backed up and Ernie grabbed the receiver.

"This is Ernie Cantrell. Who the hell is this?"

"John White Eagle, Mr. Cantrell. I hear you're looking for a buyer for Heavyweight Championship Wrestling from Florida. I'd like to come down and talk to you about it. I can catch a flight from Miami and be there in time to buy you dinner at El Meson de Pepe's. What do you say?"

Ernie watched the palm fronds dance in the breeze off the thatched tiki hut roof of the bar. He thought about walking along the beach, right where the surf meets the sand and keeps it perpetually smooth and cool, where it melts away like quicksand between your toes with each lapping of the surf.

"Mr. Cantrell?"

John would probably be a good choice, Ernie thought. He had the hustle, the fire in the belly that Ernie just didn't have anymore. He was firmly rooted in Florida wrestling's history, but young enough to see around the corner too. And he'd always been a standup guy to work with through the years.

"Mr. Cantrell, are you there?"

He remembered the first time he heard about John White Eagle. He was wrestling real live alligators as part of some outlaw promotion down in the swamps. What a great gimmick. Ernie snapped him up.

"Mr. Cantrell, are you alright?"

But the whole point of coming down here, taking a little vacation for the first time in probably forty years, was to get away from wrestling, away from these decisions, and away from the goddamn phone.

"You're not talking to the Naples Playboy, are you, Mr. Cantrell?"

"Goodbye, Johnny." Ernie gently put the receiver back in the cradle, took a good pull on his beer and watched a lone pelican skim the water's surface as he glided across the skyline.

He motioned the young bartender over. When he got there, Ernie took a hold of his shirt collar and pulled him in so they were practically nose to nose.

"No more calls," he said.

CHAPTER 71

IN ALL HIS years at *World Wrestling Digest,* Howie had never covered a wedding before. But, when a three-time World Heavyweight Champion marries the reigning Women's Champion, that's wrestling news any way you slice it.

The location? The Don Cesar. The pink castle. Gorpp remembered fondly the wedding he'd seen there. And the Tampa Bay area was where it had all started for them, in wrestling, in love. There was a through line that connected that place to their lives today, when they would become husband and wife.

Gorpp, of course, couldn't provide the necessary paperwork to get a marriage license in Florida. But the wedding meant big business for hotels, restaurants, gas stations, the media and the entire machinery of Florida's tourism-based economy. Suffice to say, there was enough money at stake to grease the tracks and turn a couple blind eyes, so the paperwork turned out not to be an issue.

Even as he wrote his copy, Howie was gobsmacked when he thought about how much Gorpp's origins had become a non-story. Good thing he wasn't really here to take over, Howie thought, 'cause we'd be easy pickings.

Gabby was adorned for her wedding as a bridal incantation of Firefly. Always playing to the cameras, those two. They had great instincts. They had the ceremony on the beach so fans could be there. As much as they were good showmen, the bride and groom also took seriously their responsibilities to be role models and ambassadors.

Howie milled around the crowd before the ceremony got underway. There were appetizers and an open bar. Pricey. Howie grabbed a couple goat cheese bites and a chili lime shrimp cup and started looking for VIPs. He snapped a shot of Dimitri and Alexi chatting with Coach Becker. Howie looked around as if he expected Bear Claw to crash the wedding and continue his assault on Dimitri. When he noticed Dimitri's nephew standing behind him, he sure hoped that wasn't on the agenda. But he wouldn't have put it past the two wrestlers tying the knot.

He saw Ernie standing quietly off to the side. Alone. Smoking a cigarette. Smooth Steve Levey had a lovely young lady on his arm and another chatting his ear off. Must be nice, Howie thought, scratching his remaining puff of white hair.

John White Eagle was gladhanding and passing out business cards for a new venture he had going. Later, Howie learned the new venture was the grand reopening of the Southeast territory. He'd picked it up for a song in an IRS auction of Earl Kruddup, Jr.'s assets. He kept Carol and Chip on to help run the operation since he spent most of his time in Miami. They practically ran the territory out of Hart's Fried Chicken for a while. White Eagle also picked up Junior's Cadillac in the auction. The official company car of the territory became a fixture in the Hart's parking lot.

Junior wouldn't have come anyway, but he couldn't have even if he'd wanted to, since he was serving time in a minimum security federal prison camp in Birmingham. Howie ended up sending him a copy of the special wedding issue of the *Digest*.

The cake topper was Gorpp spinning Firefly around in the flying saucer. Gabby's parents came. They looked like they were either in a mild form of shock or sedated, but her father did give her away, to a space alien professional wrestler. He'd thought her running away from home had been a lot to handle. Then there was circus school. Then wrestling. Now this. He was feeling like maybe *he* should run away from home.

Neither the bride nor groom were religious, but they had both learned a lot from Bobby, so they asked him and he agreed to jump through the necessary hoops to be able to officiate their wedding. Overalls watched the coverage on the sports channel. It would have been too difficult to explain his presence. *Kayfabe*. And was that really Billy Lee Riley and the Little Green Men kicking off the reception with a rousing rendition of "Flying Saucers Rock-n-Roll?"

"Hey, old man," Hank Frizzel said to Howie.

"Hey, Hank. You made it down for the big day, huh?"

"Wouldn't miss it."

"Quite a spread."

"That it is." Hank looked around at the sconces, floral arrangements and cocktail waitresses serving gourmet finger food.

"Billy Lee Riley is a nice touch too."

"Yeah? I heard this guy's really an Elvis impersonator from Sarasota but he sounds good to me."

Howie wouldn't know Billy Lee Riley from Jerry Lee Lewis, but he did know with wrestlers you could be getting worked and never even know it.

The *Star Globe's* headline read:

THE WACKY WORLD OF WRESTLING: MARTIAN MARRIAGE AND PROMOTER IN THE PEN!

They had a picture of Gorpp and Gabby waving through

the rice their guests tossed in the air as they headed for Gorpp's vessel and their honeymoon. He'd modified his transport to pass for a space-age Airstream and no one paid it much mind. The other picture in the bottom corner showed Earl Kruddup, Jr.'s perp walk from Benjamin Flowers' Ford to the Mobile, Alabama Federal Courthouse. Carol was there to snap a picture just for herself. A keepsake. She couldn't tell if Junior had seen her, but she had seen him. That was enough.

The newlyweds had just about made it through the gauntlet of fans, friends, reporters and rubberneckers. There were cans tied to the back of his vessel. It said JUST MARRIED in removable paint on the back window.

Gorpp put his arm around Gabby and gave her a squeeze. He whispered in her ear, "Remember when I said I had a solution for you leaving your vehicle for Dimitri's nephew?" He looked to his vessel.

"I don't know how," she said.

"It's easy. I'll show you."

"I do love to drive," she said.

"Hey," Howie shouted, "where you two lovebirds going on your honeymoon? Wrestling fans wanna know!"

Gorpp looked at Gabby and she giggled before shouting an answer back to Howie Shows and climbing in the driver's seat.

"Parts unknown!"

CHAPTER 72

GABRIELLE MILLER HAD NEVER BEEN to Las Vegas before. She craned her head out the window of the cab from McCarran International so she could see all the sights up and down Las Vegas Boulevard before they turned in to the circular drive in front of Caesars Palace.

She carried only a briefcase to a small conference room with a sign on the door that read **HCW Annual** in sharpie. She strode in with confidence but before she could find a seat, one of the owners motioned to her.

"Hey, sweetheart, get me some water, would you?"

Without hesitating, she picked up the full glass of ice water in front of another of the owners and flung it in the face of the one who'd asked.

"There you are," she said, then set the glass down and proceeded to her seat.

"Who in the hell do you think—"

"That's Gabby Miller," John White Eagle said from the other side of the squared circle of tables. "You know, Firefly."

"Well, what is she doing here?" He was sopping water from his sportscoat with a cloth napkin.

White Eagle looked at Gabby, but she just smiled.

"She's the owner of Heavyweight Championship Wrestling from Florida," he said. Her father, the good doctor, was actually a forty-percent shareholder. He didn't care for wrestling, but he loved his daughter and he'd decided to just go with it.

Sam Calvin put his head in his hands. One of the owners sitting closest to him heard him mutter, "You're killing me, Ernie." But then he lifted his head, gathered his composure and clinked his water glass with a spoon to bring the meeting to order.

"Welcome to Las Vegas," he said. "And welcome to the annual owners meeting. We have some new faces in the room today, but I'm sure they are well known to all of you from their illustrious careers in the ring. Please join me in welcoming the new owner of the Southeast territory, Mr. John White Eagle, and the new owner of the Florida territory, Mrs. Gabrielle Miller."

One of the owners leaned over to whisper to the one sitting beside him. "I guess if you marry an alien freak with no last name, you get to keep your own."

They both chuckled.

"Where did ole' Cranky Cantrell retire to anyway? He already lived in Florida." The same two chuckled again.

"He just told me someplace with no phones," Gabby said.

Neither of them laughed at that, but John White Eagle and Sam Calvin sure did.

"Wonder how Bobby feels about Ms. Miller here getting the nod over him," the owner with the wet coat said.

"He's the one who recommended her as a successor to Ernie Cantrell," White Eagle said. "Bobby discovered Firefly and he's always been one of her biggest backers."

"And it's Mrs., not Ms.," Gabby said.

"Seems to me like even with Ernie gone, Florida is still trying to steamroll the rest of the territories," someone in the back said to murmurs of approval.

White Eagle and Gabby stayed quiet. Neither saw any percentage in taking the bait. After a few tense moments, Sam Calvin moved them on to new business.

White Eagle *was* sore Ernie hadn't given him a shot to do what Kruddup had tried to do—consolidate the Florida and Southeast territories into one mega-territory—but he had a grudging respect for him picking Gabby. He also lamented the passing of the old timers who'd run the territories for most of his career in the ring. By next year's meeting in Atlantic City, Hank Frizzel and Nat Pfeifer would be gone too. Frizzel took the profits from selling to Upland South and got into real estate investing. Nat Pfeifer had a stroke and ended up in an assisted living facility run by the VA. They say he never was the same after the double cross in Mobile.

Bear Claw took over for Pfeifer in Minnesota, but he didn't make it a year before declaring bankruptcy. Dimitri tried to help at the very end, but it was too late. The newly expanded Upland South territory didn't last long either. It was the beginning of the end of the territories, of kayfabe and of the old ways of wrestling.

People like Howie Shows and John White Eagle may have been sentimental over the changes in the wrestling business, but they didn't have much company, at least not among the owners. It was the gentrification of professional wrestling, and few tears were shed for the displaced, the forgotten or the left behind.

Gabby eventually sold to John White Eagle. He held out with his Southeast territory—now including Florida—long enough to make a handsome profit when he sold to the national syndicate that controls wrestling these days. Now he works for them too, as a road agent and a mentor to the younger guys.

A bridge to the old territory days.

CHAPTER 73

"Think they're ready for wrasslin' on Enceladus?" Gabby asked Gorpp one day, as they ate lunch by the pool at the Don Cesar.

"It's a very different place," he said.

"Maybe we could bring a group of wrestlers from Earth and take them on a tour of the rings of Saturn. It probably wouldn't be much stranger for a lot of them than going to Japan."

Sometimes, he couldn't tell if she was teasing him. It wouldn't be unusual. But, sometimes she both meant what she was saying and was teasing him at the same time. Humans, it turned out, were more complex than the original reconnaissance indicated. He was pretty deadpan himself. They made a good couple.

She put her fork down, even though the crab cakes were delicious. She reached out and held his hand in hers. "Maybe it's time for a new challenge. We became the champions of my world. Maybe it's time to test our mettle on yours. Overalls could be our Steve Levey."

He looked at her intently and she could feel his pulse in her hand.

"I want to see the geysers of Enceladus. I want to go to your caverns under the sea. I want to see where you were born. Where you grew up. What parks you played at. Where you graduated high school. I wanna meet your folks."

Again. Teasing him with all of her Earth references. But meaning every word just the same. He squeezed her hand and was reminded again of how grateful he was to have her as his wife.

"Are you going to answer me?"

He took his hand away, picked up his fork and took a bite of Eggs Benedict, looked out at the surf and breathed in the salt air from the Gulf. "There's only one way to make it work," he said.

Gabby smiled and said, "kayfabe."

EPILOGUE

Ernie Cantrell was no Ernest Hemingway there in his rented bungalow in Key West. But, he'd picked up an IBM Selectric typewriter. And he had a nice ocean breeze coming in the window to scatter the scraps of paper and cigarette ashes around his desk, instead of that old oscillating fan from his windowless office at the Bayfront Armory. That was an improvement. He had a drip coffeemaker, a sturdy ceramic mug and a new carton of Salems. Perhaps best of all—no phone.

And Ernie had a story to tell.

With time to reflect, he thought about whether Gorpp was truly a being from another world.

Why he'd wanted to get into the wrestling business, Ernie had no earthly idea.

He hoped maybe one day, the newlyweds might come and pay him a visit. If they did, he would ask.

After a spending a lifetime in what some would call a golden age of professional wrestling, from the late 1930s to the late 1970s, Ernie had stories aplenty. He'd refereed, wrestled, managed, booked and promoted in his four decades in the business. There were stories to tell about it all. But the last story, the story of Gorpp the Grappler, was like no other.

Ernie took a sip of strong black coffee and a long drag on his cigarette, then let it smolder in the ashtray. He set his gnarled old hands on the keys and started to type.

Hailing from parts unknown...

THE END

SON OF BLACKBIRD
BOOK 2 IN THE GRAPPLER
CHRONICLES: AN EXCERPT

April 23, 1982

Gorpp landed his small vessel just off Duval Street in Key West, and opened the airlock. He and Gabby stepped out to a spring breeze carrying the scent of salt air and the sounds of a crowd celebrating. They walked onto the main drag and saw hundreds of people cheering for a plain looking man with glasses, a small flag in his shirt pocket and a microphone, speaking in impassioned tones in front of the Greater Key West Chamber of Commerce.

"I proclaim that Key West shall now be known as the Conch Republic," he said.

"What's going on?" Gabby said.

Gorpp didn't respond. They mingled with the crowd and the sound from the public address system carried the man's voice to them with more volume.

"We secede from the United States. We've raised our flag, given notice, and named our new government—"

"Seriously," she said. "What is going on?"

Gorpp looked at her but still didn't respond.

"We're not a fearful people. We're not a group to cringe

and whimper when Washington cracks the whip with contempt and unconcern. We're Conchs, and we've had enough!" He was really picking up a head of steam now and the crowd ate it up. Gabby noticed one person sporting a shirt that said, **WE SECEDED WHERE OTHERS FAILED**.

"Big trouble has started in much smaller places than this," the man said.

"That is true," Gorpp said to Gabby.

Gabby didn't respond. She turned to a man next to her with a shaggy beard, Hawaiian shirt, captain's hat and cigar. "What's going on here?"

"Haven't you heard?" he said. "We're seceding from the union!"

"Who is?" she said.

"Key West. From now on, we're going to be known as the Conch Republic. Mayor, I mean, Prime Minister Wardlow," he pointed to the man with the microphone, "he's standing up to The Gipper." He snorted. "Wardlow's the only politician I ever saw worth a damn. I'm glad I voted for him. How often do you get to say that?"

"I am calling on all my fellow citizens here in the Conch Republic to stand together, lest we fall apart, fall from fear, from a lack of courage, intimidation by an uncaring government whose actions show it has grown too big to care for people on a small island."

The crowd erupted. Gabby turned back to the man beside her.

"What's this all about?" she asked, still looking around, trying to make sense of a tourist town in Florida, where everyone from Ernest Hemingway to Harry Truman had taken up residence over the years, seceding from the union.

"Damn checkpoint," he said, pointing, as if she would be able to see it. "Up on US Route 1 in Florida City, you know, right there in front of Skeeter's Last Chance Saloon. They're gonna treat us like we ain't natural citizens, well then, Mayor, damnit, I mean Prime Minister Wardlow, he's sending a message to Ronnie, the Border Patrol and all them bureaucrats up in Washington, they can all go to hell. We'll be just fine on our own if that's how they're gonna treat us."

Gabby looked around again, trying to make sense of it. The energy in the crowd felt more like Mardi Gras than a revolution. People wore silly hats or swim trunks. They drank beer and Margaritas.

"What's the roadblock for? What are they looking for?"

"Some say drugs, cause it makes a good talking point for Nancy and her 'Just Say No' campaign, but what it's really about—" He stopped himself and took a good look at Gorpp for the first time, then resumed in a hushed voice, "is illegal aliens."

Gorpp and Gabby shared a look.

"Hey, wait a second," the man said. He inhaled on his cigar and pointed at Gorpp. "You're that alien wrestler guy, aren't you?"

"Yes," Gorpp said.

The man let out an I'll be damned, burst of laughter. The Prime Minister had finished his speech and a mix of reggae from a nearby bar and mariachi music from a band of street musicians mingled in the air with whoops and hollers of inebriated revelry.

The man with the beard and cigar regarded Gorpp again thoughtfully.

"You best not try to go up through that checkpoint, if you take my meaning. I mean, no offense but…" He trailed off and shrugged at Gorpp.

Gorpp didn't respond.

The crowd was starting to move around them, like a living thing. Some headed for Sloppy Joe's, a favorite haunt of Hemingway's. Some danced in the streets in drag, and some were doing media interviews with the likes of Michael Putney and even Mort Castle. The New York anchorman had jumped on an Eastern Airlines flight as soon as the rumblings of secession started. Eastern was the only airline with service to the island. Castle liked being the first national correspondent on the scene when history was unfolding, so he kept track of these kinds of things.

The man beside them brushed long and oily hair out of his eyes to reveal wraparound sunglasses.

"Don't worry, champ," he said. He looked around at the band of hippies, drag queens, artists and misfits who made up the newly formed Conch Republic. He put an earnest hand on Gorpp's shoulder. "You're gonna fit right in around here."

Gorpp didn't respond. He squeezed Gabby's hand as if to say, let's move along.

Their new friend senses his restlessness and added, "Oh wait, citizen, before you go, you want one of these cigars?" He reached into the pocket of his Hawaiian shirt. "Made right here on the island. Better then Cubans." He tucked the hand-rolled cigar into Gorpp's hand.

To Gabby's surprise, Gorpp inspected it, nimbly removed the cap with his knife-like fingernails and placed it in his mouth.

"Got a light?" he asked the man.

With a familiar motion, the man produced a butane lighter from his shirt pocket and lit Gorpp's cigar.

Gabby looked at him.

"I'm celebrating," he said.

"Long live the Conch Republic!" the man shouted, eliciting a few cheers from those in earshot. Then he turned back to the couple. "Comrades, I bid you adieu. I've got a date with a blender, some run and a balcony with a great view of the Gulf. Come to think of it, you're welcome to join me if you'd like."

"We'd love to," Gabby said. "But we've got a date of our own, with an old friend."

"May the road rise with you," he said with a flourish of his cigar, tossing his long hair out of his eyes again. He started to turn away, then said, "They call me 'Duck,' by the way. Bunch of quacks if you ask me!"

Gorpp had never displayed an appreciation for wordplay or subscribed to the human social convention of feigning an insincere response out of a sense of obligation to be courteous. Gabby offered an obligatory chuckle. Gorpp tugged on her hand again, this time more forcefully. Gabby tugged right back.

"Say, Duck, can you spare another one of those?"

"You betcha!" Duck produced another cigar for the lady but she waved off the light.

"It's for a friend," she said.

Continue reading *Son of Blackbird*.
Get the links at DRFeiler.com.

ACKNOWLEDGMENTS

I would like to thank my first readers, Jerry, Rebecca and Rowan, for their early encouragement and support. Thanks go as well to Bill, Angela and Victoria for their technical assistance along the way.

ABOUT THE AUTHOR

D.R. Feiler is a pen name for author Damien Filer whose works have appeared under many names, in publications ranging from *Pro Wrestling Illustrated* to the *New York Times*. He is the cofounder of an independent record label, a sought after speaker and an adjunct lecturer at a state university. He has appeared everywhere from Star Trek to the cover of a Stephen King novel. Damien has written a song with the lead singer of punk legends, the Bad Brains, and an award-winning script for a world heavyweight boxing champion. He is a graduate of Clarion Writers' Workshop at Michigan State University. He lives on planet Earth with his beautiful wife and daughter, two silly dogs and a bobtail cat.

Made in the USA
Columbia, SC
31 August 2022